THE EDGE
OF
THE WOOD

Short Stories

by

Alan Bold

By The Same Author

Poetry
SOCIETY INEBRIOUS
THE VOYAGE
TO FIND THE NEW
A PERPETUAL MOTION MACHINE
PENGUIN MODERN POETS 15 (With Morgan & Brathwaite)
THE STATE OF THE NATION
THE AULD SYMIE
HE WILL BE GREATLY MISSED
A CENTURY OF PEOPLE
A PINT OF BITTER
SCOTLAND, YES
THIS FINE DAY
A CELTIC QUINTET (With Bellany)
IN THIS CORNER: SELECTED POEMS 1963-83
HAVEN (With Bellany)

Stories
HAMMER AND THISTLE (With Morrison)

Criticism
THOM GUNN & TED HUGHES
GEORGE MACKAY BROWN
THE BALLAD
THE SENSUAL SCOT
MODERN SCOTTISH LITERATURE
MACDIARMID: THE TERRIBLE CRYSTAL
TRUE CHARACTERS (With Giddings)

As Editor
THE PENGUIN BOOK OF SOCIALIST VERSE
THE MARTIAL MUSE: SEVEN CENTURIES OF WAR POETRY
THE CAMBRIDGE BOOK OF ENGLISH VERSE 1939-75
MAKING LOVE: THE PICADOR BOOK OF EROTIC VERSE
THE BAWDY BEAUTIFUL: THE SPHERE BOOK OF IMPROPER VERSE
MOUNTS OF VENUS: THE PICADOR BOOK OF EROTIC PROSE
DRINK TO ME ONLY: THE PROSE (AND CONS) OF DRINKING
SMOLLETT: AUTHOR OF THE FIRST DISTINCTION
THE SEXUAL DIMENSION IN LITERATURE
A SCOTTISH POETRY BOOK
SCOTT: THE LONG-FORGOTTEN MELODY
BYRON: WRATH AND RHYME
THE THISTLE RISES: A MACDIARMID MISCELLANY
MACDIARMID: AESTHETICS IN SCOTLAND
THE LETTERS OF HUGH MACDIARMID

THE EDGE
OF
THE WOOD

Alan Bold

They watch them, they watch as they walk
To the lodge on the edge of the wood
Filling the silence with starry talk
As those linked together should.

'Markinch Triptych'

LUATH PRESS Ltd.
Barr, Ayrshire.

First Published in 1984
By Luath Press Ltd.,
Barr, Ayrshire.

The Publisher acknowledges subsidy from the Scottish Arts Council towards the publication of this volume.

The end-piece to each story in this volume is an Illumination, much enlarged, taken from The Book Of Kells.

TO JOHN BETT

in another part of the wood

ACKNOWLEDGEMENTS

'Post Mortem' was first published in *The Scotsman;* 'The Recluse' appeared in *The Malahat Review* and was broadcast as a BBC Morning Story; 'The Earth House at Crabwick Farm', 'The Ferret', 'See You' and 'Black Hole' were included in issues of *Scotia Review.* I am most grateful to the editors concerned for their encouragement in the first place. I must thank my wife, Alice, for enhancing the text with her imaginative illustrations; and Tom Scott for introducing the collection in an illuminating way.

A.B.

CONTENTS

INTRODUCTION by Tom Scott I
Foreword V
1. The Recluse 1
2. Post Mortem 7
3. The Earth House At Crabwick Farm 17
4. The Vandals 26
5. The Ferret 32
6. A Scottish Zhivago 40
7. The Pygmalion Pill 43
8. The First Poem 54
9. The Candlemaker's Dream 62
10. See You 69
11. The Cock and Bull Story 75
12. A Dog's Life 93
13. Black Hole 112
14. The Vegetable 117
15. You'd Need To Be A Saint 125
16. The Day Of The Gael 131
17. A Portrait Of The Artist As Anstruther Man 144
18. Broken Octaves 154
19. The Early Life Of Dolly Silver 160

THE BLEW BLANKET LIBRARY

The *Blew* (or Blue) *Blanket* was the privileged insignia of the craftsmen of Edinburgh in the time of James III. It was pledged to them by Privy Seal in 1482 when the craftsmen of the city, together with the Merchants and other loyal subjects, marched on Edinburgh Castle and freed their King. It remained their insignia for centuries, and one of the original Blew Blankets is today in the Museum of Antiquities in Edinburgh.

The *Blew Blanket Library* is a collection of new books on Scotland by Scottish writers. Its aim is to provide a forum where writer-craftsmen of all types can display their goods in the context of Scotland today.

INTRODUCTION

There is a tale that once an old Chinese philosopher decided to write a representative biography of a man.   He wrote over a million words, then read what he had written down.   It seemed to him rather long, so he began to pare it down to essentials.   The more he pared, the more he saw to pare.   At last it seemed to him that he got it right, and he looked at the finished oeuvre.   It read: *He was born, he lived, he died.*

That perhaps is taking the art of the short story to extremes of condensation, but the principle is unfaultable.   A story can be of epic length or only a few syllables.   The short story is more short than story.   One of the greatest stories of all time is the reputed message of Caesar from Britain to Rome: *I came, I saw, I won.*   In Latin it is merely six syllables: *veni, vidi, vici.*   Like many short stories it is also a slice of life, a piece of reality — it is true.   It would be no less so if someone other than Caesar reported of him: *He came, he saw, he won.*   At base we have simply the form of the sentence — a subject about which something is predicated.   The shortest sentence in the Bible is also the shortest story: *Jesus wept.*   If one adds to that *'for Lazarus',* you augment the tale, complete it, but you add nothing to the essence, for it is implied that Jesus did not weep without good cause, from his own point of view.

I

It is worth reminding ourselves of these facts, for the modern short story from Poe and Gogol through many great writers of many lands gives us a bewildering wealth of specimens. What has the short story of Poe in common with that of D.H. Lawrence or H.E. Bates? That of Maupassant with that of Fred Urquhart or Grassic Gibbon? That of Henry James with that of Hemingway or O Henry? Many varieties of story have been shaped not by any literary necessity but by mere fashion, a magazine editor's whim, or that of of his readers. I remember L.A.G.Strong saying that he complained to a U.S. publishing tycoon, over the 'ceegaurs' after an opulent dinner, that none of his editors ever accepted an L.A.G. Strong story. The tycoon removed his 'ceegaur' and said: 'Son, there A hundred and one reasons why an editor reejects a story: but not one of these is A liderairy reason.'

Faced with this problem of what kind of story and what kind of style, and lamenting a vital market to be dominated by, Alan Bold simply goes back to the beginning, the short story as told in the street, in the pub, at mothers' meetings or the like — to gossip, in short. It is from the simple anecdote that the genre takes off, and to that it returns for renewal. Many of the stories told here are drawn from a small township in Fife which Alan Bold calls Marshend: he himself lives in Markinch. They smack of the reality of small town life, its virtues of simplicity and homeliness, its vices of narrowness and cruelty. The first story in the book, *The Recluse*, has more than a little of the pure folktale in it, the easy interplay of the natural and the supernatural, and for all I know may be a version of some local legend that the author has picked up in conversation.

Post Mortem is more in the nature of some local real event, a horror story, than of folklore —in this case a double murder and its outcome. The contrast between the quiet, sleepy surface of the little township and the grim underlying reality unfolded by the tale will not surprise those who know anything about small-town Scottish life. This grim note is struck again in *The Earth-house at Crabwick Farm*,

II

this time involving an elderly couple of holiday-makers: but here the very nature of the place seems to evoke the murderous hate which the tale reveals. The same grim reality makes *The Vandals* a nightmare of mindless oppression of a solitary old man —the theme of solitude seeking solitude in a peaceful environment is a main one in these tales —which has appalling consequences. Mr. Bold's Marshend is more than a little reminiscent of George Douglas's Barbie, though in no way derivative, and like George Douglas he has an eye for the depths of evil that can underlie a deceptively benign surface.

One of the things about a small town is that it is apt to be a death-trap for its own young people: they have nothing to do, no industry on a big enough scale to absorb them all into jobs, the future is a blank wall. Some may escape to work in larger towns outside, or emigrate, but for most it may be a slow living death of unemployment, poverty, deprivation physical and spiritual. In such a scene lives decay, become destructive of self and others. So in *The Ferret*, as in *The Vandals,* we see the corrupting effects of such a life on youth: hopelessness leading to corruption.

Earlier stories I have read by Alan Bold were drawn from his life in Edinburgh, and some of the best of the present collection are autobiographical (so I guess), or drawn from his Edinburgh experience. Thus, *A Scottish Zhivago* is about the pathos of film-fantasy getting mixed up with real life, and *The First Poem* is a delightful story of the sixteen-year old poet trying to act up to a woman twice his age, leading to the writing of his first poem. And one of the best stories in the book, *A Portrait of the Artist as Anstruther Man,* I take also to be autobiographical. Lewis MacBeth is a marvellous character, no doubt drawn from life, and his adventures behind the Iron Curtain are comedy of a high order.

These Marshend, Edinburgh and autobiographical tales however give no idea of the variety of this collection. There is a story about a man who invents a *Pygmalion Pill* by which an inarticulate workman is changed into a smooth-talking manager: one about a spaceman's adventure with a Black Hole: one about a being from an outer planet who pretends to be a hospital living vegetable to get some insight into human life. And even among the village tales we have such imaginative flights as *The Candlemakers' Dream* and *The Cock and Bull Story*. All in all a remarkable range of themes, subjects, character, plots, slices of life. But I have said enough, and it is time for the Prologue to step aside : RING UP THE CURTAIN.

Tom Scott

FOREWORD

According to various sources, the short story is no longer a viable literary form. Readers demand, so certain authorities assert, the sustained dimension of time associated with the novel. Although there are certainly fewer outlets for the short story in the 1980s, the form nevertheless persists and, in Scotland especially, has a healthy contemporary life as well as a glorious literary past. George Mackay Brown, Fred Urquhart and Muriel Spark — to name only three Scottish writers — have shown how much emotion can be contained in a relatively brief span.

One of these writers — Fred Urquhart in his Introduction to *Modern Scottish Short Stories* (1978) — contends that the Scottish short story derives from the tradition of the popular ballad (as collected by Child, not sung by Sinatra). Certainly there are similarities: the desire to plunge immediately into action; the use of dialogue to convey character; the determination to let events speak for themselves without moralistic comment. There is, however, another factor.

Scotland thrives on gossip. At any gathering — in the pub or on the football terraces or even under the sheets — there is a story to be told. Scots love to tell tales, often with the rough cutting edge of the tongue: so-and-so did that; do you know what thingumay did the other night; you should have seen, you should have heard, etc. This love of gossip is, I believe, what motivates the Scottish short story — at least as much as a folk memory of the ballads.

As a poet I am accustomed to shaping experience into a definite form: using literary discipline to restrain naturally expansive impulses. In my short stories I have tried to convey several moods and moments in narratives displaying some of the spontaneity we respond to in the finest examples of Scottish gossip. I hope I have made this clear in these stories.

Alan Bold

THE RECLUSE

THE RECLUSE

Robert Ellis, a man past fifty, had acquired the habit over many years of depending entirely on his own resources. Actually his financial resources were inherited from his widower-father, a preposterously hard-working man who had — through initial industry and a subsequent genius for investment — accumulated a tidy fortune for the benefit of his only son. This money did not make Ellis an egregiously wealthy man able to splash money around like jugs of warm water. It did mean he could live his entire life in a state of leisurely security; as Ellis had never taken a wife he did not even need to worry about bestowing the paternal inheritance on the fruits of marital procreation. Ellis's life was like the last page of an open book. All he had to do was bide his time (reading assiduously between the lines) and he would eventually, and without much incident, come to a satisfactory end. For he had no superstitious fear of death; his demise, when it came, would simply be a conclusion.

Ellis had no curiosity at all about his fellow mortals and no wish to mix with them. He lived in a small cottage in a rural part of Scotland and had all his needs — including food and fuel — delivered to his door before paying for them by cheque. Thus his only obligation was to make the occasional stroll down to the postbox on the edge of a main road that bypassed the makeshift road that led to and from his cottage. He was quite alone and perfectly content in his isolation. Sometimes a passerby would knock on the door to ask for a direction, but Ellis would not answer the irrelevant summons. He felt his cottage was his castle and that he owed the outside world precisely nothing.

Apart from reading the books he obtained by subscribing to book clubs the only interest Ellis allowed himself was passive observation. He had purchased, by mail order, a fine pair of binoculars (35 by 10) and with these he could get a closer view of the world his little bit of earth revolved around. He could watch the crows spinning round the tops of the pine trees or set his sights on the erratic behaviour of a bullfinch. At night he would stand outside his cottage and scan the skies, watching for hours at a time the configurations of Orion with its red star Betelgeuse a particular attraction. Certainly the sky interested him vastly more than the folk who lived in the nearest village. Their distance of two miles seemed like several light-years away from his consciousness.

To the north of his cottage, high on a hill, there was a farm. Ellis had glanced at the white-painted farmhouse and the rust-coloured barns from time to time and, during his nocturnal observations, had been irritated by the light that shone — like an unknown orange star — from the nearest window of the farmhouse. As for the people within, he did not care to be bothered by them. One cloudy night in late January he had no luck with his heavenly perusals and turned his eyes, and his binoculars, to the hazy orange light emanating from the farmhouse. It was extremely faint to the naked eye and scarcely less so even with the aid of powerful binoculars. Yet the place held his attention that night. When he retired to his single bed he thought, uncharacterisically, how that light seemed unattainable in contrast with the welcome light of the usual stars. They were securely up there even though they swam through the skies with the passing of the seasons. They were familiar; the light from the farmhouse was incredibly remote.

Next morning the mist had cleared and Ellis decided to have a closer look at the buildings on the hill. He reached for his binoculars and focused them expertly. He could see small human figures standing in front of the farmhouse, could see them as general shapes though he could not read their facial features. They were moving in a random manner, now converging, now scattering in various directions. Ellis could not justify to himself this sudden interest in these ongoings, but he watched for around half an hour before he told himself that this must stop. These people had nothing to do with him, he with them. He rationalized that he had been disappointed the previous night when atmospheric conditions had made star-gazing impossible and that he had unconsciously let his mind slip sideways to the people who lived so near and so far from him.

Fortunately that night the sky was gloriously clear and Ellis began contentedly to survey its black pointed beauty. Instinctively he began at Orion, that majestic marker, and moved his binoculars down to the brilliant Sirius then up again to Aldebaron (the eye of the bull) then on to the jewel-studded cluster of the Pleiades. He was lost in his thoughts again — happy. He contemplated the astonishing fact that the pinpoints of light he was looking at had taken millions of years to reach him, that he was visually probing deep into the universal past. Then he swept up into the Milky Way, the centre of his galaxy, and began to cogitate on the myriad of stars that shone there seemingly for him alone. Then, as if possessed, he turned to face the north, lowered his sights, and watched the light from the farmhouse. He felt a visceral sense of disgust as if after all those years he had lost his serene self-control. He packed his binoculars and retreated back into his house for a troubled night's sleep.

The following days passed in some confusion. Ellis tried desperately hard to obliterate the farmhouse from his mind but caught himself staring over at it from time to time and cursing himself for doing so. It had become an unwelcome intrusion on his mental privacy. Yet there was no reason whatsoever for this obsession. Being a man of some determination, Ellis decided that he would observe the farmhouse at regular intervals for an entire day and that, having accomplished his self-imposed task, he would be free from the niggling irritation of that hillside forever and could go back to his astronomical and ornithological interests.

On the designated day Ellis rose early, at dawn, and looked through his binoculars at the farmhouse. Minimal activity — people stirring, popping in and out of the house, generally doing little with a lot of show as if someone (not Ellis) was watching them. At midday Ellis noted that nothing much had changed but, as the day got into its stride, he felt a compulsion to shift his centre of interest to the right of the farm complex. He shrugged his shoulders and tracked down the hill until his gaze stopped on a large square stone building which, to his certain knowledge, he had not noticed before. It was obviously a very old building, but not a complete ruin. Nevertheless there was nothing happening there, nothing at all. It just stood on the slope leading down from the farm and some sheep grazed in the field in front of it. It was difficult to get a really detailed image of the building because, unless the sunlight picked out the lightest stones, it blended in with the trees immediately behind it.

Ellis was satisfied. Now he could provide himself with a logical explanation of the source of his irritant. He reasoned that when he had previously glanced at the hillside his vision was disturbed because it could not completely take in all the facets of the spectacle. He had not consciously seen the old building but had somehow taken cognizance of it. Thereafter his unconscious mind had insisted on finding out the whole truth. Now that he knew exactly where the building was he could pick it out at will during the daytime. At night, of course, it was totally invisible. Even by a full moonlight.

For weeks after this solution had presented itself to him Ellis felt he could ignore the hillside. His life succumbed comfortably to his previous routine. He was content to be on his own and not to have outside distractions imposed on him against his will. Thus, on a sunny afternoon, as if to prove he could casually take in the hillside in his binocular vision, he focused on it. He was instantly dumbfounded. There, unmistakably, on the top right hand corner of the old building — which must have stood at least thirty feet high — was a child. Just sitting, perched there. How he had got there Ellis could not imagine unless there were stairs behind the wall that he was observing.   At any rate it seemed an astonishing phenomenon.   He looked as hard as he could and though he could not pick out the boy's face he had the impression that the clothes he was wearing were rags.   This disturbed and shook him.   He had an impulse to rush across the fields and investigate before his old determination to make nothing human any of his business intervened.   He would leave the boy to his precarious poverty.   Whoever he was could not affect Robert Ellis.

The cottage inhabited by Ellis lay in a valley bounded to the north by the enigmatic hillside and strong winds would swoop around the cottage wall and rustle through the adjacent trees.   Ellis was well used to eerie noises by night.   But the night after he had seen the boy he was appalled to hear another noise entirely: the noise, distant but distinct, of a boy singing.   He could not decipher the words but it was not a moan; it was a song, a dirge, a lament.   Ellis retreated to his cottage then emerged again to make sure.   There it was, still, like a melodic sob hanging on the air.   The sound of a child chanting.

By this time, thoroughly unsettled by what he had seen and heard, Ellis decided to make enquiries into the history of the old building. He wrote off to the local librarian for a list of books on local history and, having obtained the information, sent for and received the relevant titles.   In one of them, *An Annotated Inventory of Antiquities,* he found this passage:

There is a story concerning the old Keep adjoining Skinner's Farm.   This Keep is all that remains of a fifteenth-century castle once owned by a certain Colonel.   Among the Colonel's household was an orphan boy who infuriated his employer by his incessant singing.   Once, sorely provoked by the lad's singing, the Colonel rebuked him and to teach him a lesson locked him in the Keep.   Preoccupied by pressing family problems, the Colonel forgot about the boy for a week.   To his horror, when he opened the Keep he discovered that the child had died of starvation. The little boy lay with his mouth open as if singing a last terrible song. Shortly after this the Colonel's affairs were the subject of an official enquiry and his estate was ruined. Since then the local folk have avoided the Keep by night lest the ghost of the boy should walk. One old woman, who worked on Skinner's Farm, claimed that she saw the boy sitting on the walls of the Keep one morning singing one of his favourite songs.

Doubtless the anecdote is apocryphal but the story of Robert Ellis's experience is a true one and the legend of the singing boy is still current in local folklore. I know that because I moved into the cottage after Ellis's death and found an account of his sighting neatly preserved in the diary he left behind him. What use Ellis made of his discovery is not recorded by him, though I know from the locals that he remained a recluse. Probably he went on much as he had before, kept looking through his binoculars at the birds by day and stars by night. Possibly he stared at the hillside from time to time. The narrative of the singing boy is the last thing he wrote in his diary for he died, of a heart seizure, several months after that last entry.

The only thing I can add is what the local doctor (a man as fond of a good gossip as he is of a good drink) told me. Namely, that the cessation of Ellis's regular cheques aroused suspicion that something had happened to this punctilious man; that the police and, naturally, the doctor were summoned. This same doctor claims he found Ellis, on the floor, with his mouth open as if singing. I'm inclined to dismiss this as incidental elaboration of a simple death from natural causes. After all, the hillside is still there, as is the farm and Keep. I have Ellis's binoculars — all his things came as part and parcel of the cottage — and have looked and looked at the hillside and seen nothing but what is there. Nothing but the farm and the old building to the right and the trees behind and the sky beyond. I can see them now.

POST MORTEM

In a little rural town people talk a lot, that's their nature. When something out of the ordinary happens in a little rural town people talk a lot more than they should do. Such, at any rate, is my conclusion after living through the events I am about to describe. It is not a pleasant story but it happened nevertheless. I can only hope that the exposure of the facts might prevent something of this nature happening again. I can only hope.

I became involved in the affair because I had decided, after retiring from general practice, to live in the country away from the hectic bustle of a big city. Often enough I had prescribed rest and fresh air as the perfect cure for fatigue, and when the time came for me to retire I felt I should take my own advice. I had spent a lifetime listening to other people's problems, diagnosing their aches and pains, generally lending a helping hand. It was the nature of my profession that I only saw people in times of trouble — mental or physical, sometimes a combination of both. As a result I had a rather jaundiced view of city people. There were young malingerers who suddenly contracted an illness — an illness unknown to medicine usually — when they wanted a few days off work; there were the old people who were never happy unless they had something wrong with them. I had been born in the country and knew that country folk were mentally and physically more robust than their urban counterparts. I therefore felt I should spend my last years cultivating a nice garden as well as a sense of wellbeing.

The little rural town I chose, Marshend, seemed ideal. It had a small population and a papermaking factory provided employment for the locals. There was no unemployment problem, no bored youths hanging around street corners. When I told my colleagues I was going to live in Marshend they invariably said *'But nothing ever happens there'* — which confirmed my judgement. That was where I wanted to be — a place where nothing ever happened. Thus I bought a handsome cottage on the edge of a wood in Marshend and began my quiet rural life putting my garden in order. I had been a widower for many years, had never had any children, so felt at peace on my own, felt happy with isolation. If I wanted company I could always go down to the local inn and linger over a glass of malt whisky. Otherwise I kept myself to myself.

I had been in Marshend for about a month when I became aware of something unusual. As I took my morning walk for my daily paper I saw two elderly women talking excitedly in the street. It punctured the quiet of the quiet little town. It was a cold wintry day and the wind carried the words of the women and amplified them. They seemed oblivious to my passing presence as I walked slowly so I could catch the gist of a conversation that was somehow too intense for Marshend. I heard them clearly.

'He made a real spectacle of himself. You should have seen him. He was shouting and bawling in the street and the tears were streaming from his eyes.'

'I heard from people who live in the next stair that the noise was something terrible. He's usually such a miserable creature, never says anything to anybody. Though they say he was howling and yelling and screaming and cursing. Screaming blue murder. The noise was something terrible.'

'Well, it will have to stop. Someone will have to say something.'

'True. That's true.'

Instantly I had an image in my mind of some poor old chap who, just once in his life, had taken too much to drink and had made an idiot of himself in the street. In a city nobody would have turned a hair. But here this little incident took on the proportions of a major scandal. I felt for the man though I had no idea who he was. I imagined him coming out the morning after the night before, full of guilt and remorse, and getting cold looks and frigid frowns for his trouble. Would he ever recover from the brunt of their moral indignation? Well, it was none of my business. I went into the shop and bought my paper. When I came out the women were still at it and I shivered a bit at the peak their maliciousness had reached.

'Did you know he had blood on his hands? Said he'd been out killing rabbits. I ask you —killing rabbits at that time of night!'

'A likely story!'

I quickened my pace and looked forward to getting back to my cottage. I had been up early to make a log fire and when I got back it was blazing. It was now my habit, every morning, to make a cup of coffee, light a pipe and sit by the fire to read the paper. If nothing ever happened in Marshend I still wanted to know, from the safe distance of my armchair, what was happening in the rest of the world. I rubbed my hands in front of my fire. Outside the wind could blow, but I was snug. I looked at the window — at the bleak fields and evergreen trees through it, then at the basket of logs beneath it. In summer those fields would be swarming with sheep. Now they were empty except for a few rabbits that darted out from time to time. I made my coffee. And I settled down with my newspaper.

I saw that the world was at its usual. There were wars and revolutions and strikes and pay claims and unemployment and the rest of it. It was the same every day. All that bustle out there in the big world made my little haven even more heavenly. I relaxed, then suddenly started as an item caught my eye. In the column reserved for '*Latest News*' — usually a blank space — there was a paragraph set in red ink. A story about Marshend. It was headed 'MARSHEND MURDER' and said the unthinkable in a couple of sentences: '*Police are investigating a murder in the town of Marshend. A young girl was found dead early this morning in Missionary Woods. Local police are handling the case.*'

I almost dropped my pipe in astonishment. Missionary Woods — that was the wood that skirted my cottage. It was called Missionary Woods because, according to local tradition, an obscure missionary was supposed to have planted the first tree there. I virtually lived in the wood, the path that reached the heart of it passed my front door. Nothing ever happened in Marshend, and now here I was reading about the murder of a young girl, a murder that had taken place almost on my doorstep. It seemed like a nightmare. I didn't have long to wait for further news about the murder. Around noon two policemen arrived — a huge one and a surprisingly small one.

'You are new to Marshend?'

'Yes, that is correct.'

'You know we must ask you some questions?'

'Yes, I read about the girl.'

They looked at my newspaper for a meaningful thirty seconds then ask the questions they did. Where was I at 11pm the previous night? When did I usually go to bed? Did I hear anything peculiar? Did I see anything out of the ordinary? What time did I wake up? Did I know the murdered girl? Of course I could tell them nothing at all. I had heard nothing. But they stayed half an hour asking questions. When they had finished I felt I had to ask a question of my own.

'How do you know the girl was murdered? As a doctor — retired now — I have a professional interest. I'm not asking out of mere curiosity.'

The tall policeman looked at his small colleague, cleared his throat, then looked straight at me.

'The girl, young Brenda Thomson, was found with her throat cut and her arms and her legs had been bound.'

Although I had seen and heard many things as a doctor I felt quite nauseated. Murder was always a foul affair but most murders were hotheaded extensions of domestic squabbles. This, however, was a really nasty piece of work, a premeditated act of slaughter.

'I hope you catch whoever did this,' I told the policemen.

'We will', said the big one. 'He can't be very far away.'

I pondered on the significance of this last remark as I saw the policemen to the door. It seemed odd of them to think the crime had been committed by a local. To me it seemed much more likely to be the act of an escaped homicidal maniac passing through. An aberrant act. A ghastly mistake.

As the days passed the mood in the little town became more and more oppressive. Gone was the atmosphere of tranquillity. Gone the quiet evenings in the inn over a glass of malt whisky. Instead everyone talked about the murder, everyone said they knew who had done it. The culprit, so the locals said, was a middle-aged man called James Turner who worked as a butcher in the town. He was also, I soon discovered, the man the two old women had been talking about outside the paper shop. Many of the local people had seen, or heard, him on the night of the murder, staggering home in an outrageous state, screaming and shouting and with blood on his hands. The town had judged him and found him guilty.

Because of the consensus of gossip in the town this man Turner was picked up and questioned by the police. The town heaved a sigh of relief confident that the murderer had been apprehended. But the police released Turner. The blood, they explained, came from rabbits. There was no case against him. Apparently it was Turner's habit to hunt rabbits at night. It was his way of making a little money on the side. He would go into the wood in the dark with a torch and knife. He would shine the torch from side to side until he caught a rabbit in the glare. Then, with the animal transfixed and rooted to the spot, he would club it dead and —expert with a knife that he was — would butcher it on the spot. It was gruesome, but no crime. Sometimes he caught as many as a dozen rabbits a night and he would sell these on the side.

Unfortunately for James Turner he was extremely unpopular in the little town.   The good folk of Marshend thought it indecent for a man to be walking around with a torch and a butcher's knife at the dead of night.   He had become a sort of bogeyman for children.   *'Jimmy Turner will get you!'* was a phrase to strike terror into the hearts of children.   And he was no figment of the imagination.   People saw him every day.   Repulsive in appearance, he was bald and unshaven and walked with a sinister stoop.   But the worst thing about him was the relish with which he cut up butcher meat.   He stood surrounded by raw animal carcases and when someone wanted a part of a beast he would thud the carcase onto his big marble slab and hack at it with maniacal relish.   At least, this is what the locals told me.

So James Turner was the man the town suspected, no matter what the police might decide.   He looked the part and, with his connexion with blood and cutting, seemed the logical choice.   The town added to this evidence the fact that James Turner was an unmarried man who lived on his own and that in itself seemed odd.   When he went to the inn he would drink by himself in a corner and respond to the occasional 'Good Evening' with a cold stare.   Yes, James Turner fitted the part of the villain.

On the day of his release the psychological temperature of the town was at boiling point.   The good folk of Marshend could not accept that Turner's release signified his innocence.   Personally I thought that even though the man was innocent — and he surely was — he would do better to leave the little town.   Better to go than stay, for the stain of guilt by general acclamation would stick to him like the blood from one of his butchered carcases.   Before the murder he had been a loner by choice.   Now he would not find a friend if he paid for one.

Two weeks passed, then a month, then two months.   Still nobody had been charged with the murder of Brenda Thomson.   Turner remained in the town but lost his job in the butcher's shop.   The good folk would not buy meat that had been touched by his inhuman hands. So Turner tried to keep out of the way. He even travelled to another village to buy his groceries as nobody in Marshend would serve him. He had become Public Enemy Number One in Marshend. A hideous spectacle to be avoided. I was aware of the injustice of it all but could do nothing about it. As an incomer to Marshend I had been received with courtesy and was not about to make the remaining days of my life unbearable by speaking up for Turner.

I soon settled back into my quiet way of life, buying my newspaper, sitting by my log fire, reading a good book. The affair gradually drifted out of my consciousness — until one evening, the most unforgettable evening of my life.

I was dozing by the fire and it was around 11pm when I was startled by the sound of a crowd nearby. I was amazed at the volume of noise, for usually the place was deadly quiet. At first I thought I was dreaming but, no, there were distinct sounds, people shouting and someone screaming. If I had had a 'phone I would have contacted the police, but one of my comforts in my retirement was the absence of a telephone, the instrument that had incessantly screamed at me during my days as a doctor. I had no alternative but to investigate the noise.

Opening my front door I saw a crowd of people from the town, people I recognised. There was the innkeeper, the man who sold me newspapers, the two old women, housewives, workers, almost everyone, it seemed. They all had torches and were formed in a solid crowd with a man in front of them. There was no mistaking who that man was — Turner. I saw, in the torchlight, his stooping figure and as the light flashed over his face I watched him shouting and screaming. For he could do nothing else — his wrists were bound and the leaders of the crowd were preparing to bind his feet. There was nothing I could do to help him. I just stood transfixed, rooted to the spot, like the rabbits that Turner had hunted and killed.

13

And I watched as they killed him. Yes, they killed Turner. There in the woods, virtually on my doorstep, on the spot where the young girl had been murdered. As I watched, the ritual significance this killing had for the townspeople became clear to me. They felt that this man had eluded justice and they were going to make sure he got his just desserts. They were like a lynch mob. They took a butcher's knife and they cut his throat and they watched as he fell to the ground and as the dark blood pumped out of him and he died in the torchlight.

I left Marshend after that. One murder was bad enough, God knows, but to actually witness a ritual slaughter was altogether more than I could bear to live with. Of course, I followed the progress of the case in the newspapers. The police took the nature of Turner's death —identical to the manner of Brenda Thomson's — as clear evidence that there was a mass murderer at large who might repeat his methods. Because the case was now of national concern the big police guns were called in to solve it and solve it they did. They found out that the murderer of Brenda Thomson was none other than her father, a quiet unasssuming man who had simply gone insane. There was no doubt about it and Mr. Thomson confessed in detail. Once the police had that confession they put two and two together and alleged that Mr. Thomson had also killed James Turner. The two crimes were clearly the work of the one man. Thomson was jailed for life, the case was closed. What the police could never understand was why Thomson, who was willing to admit to the killing of his own daughter, refused to confess to the murder of Turner.

I knew, but said nothing. I wanted to put the memory of that terrible night out of my mind. I wanted my retirement to be a time of peace. Yet I could never forget the slaughter that took place before my eyes that night. Which is why, ten years later, I am telling the story. Had I told it before it would not have helped Thomson — who deserved to be put away anyway. I'm told that Marshsend is still a quiet little village where people go to retire and, as I haven't long to live now, I want to tell this tale so people going through my papers will find out the truth.   And when they find out they will talk.   And the talk will get to Marshend.   And I want it to, because it was their talk that killed James Turner.   And perhaps, just perhaps, my silence.

THE EARTH HOUSE
AT CRABWICK FARM

THE EARTH HOUSE AT CRABWICK FARM

Mr. and Mrs. Huntingdon had come to the little island for a restful holiday. He, because he worked hard all the year round. She, because she decided she needed a rest. So with the mimimum of dissension they booked up on a car ferry and were transported over the sea to the little island. They were completely inconspicious on board, particularly Mr. Huntingdon who had a decidedly unfair share of the eleven feet three inches their collective height amounted to. Besides, Mrs. Huntingdon did not choose to mingle with other passengers.

At their age there was little appeal in continental binges full of punishing hangovers and hazy memories of evenings spent indulging in expensively romantic corner cafes. They had never passed through that age. At their age there was a shared desire for peace and quiet, for isolation and reflection — so Mrs. Huntingdon said. So she had chosen the little island with its neolithic monuments and turbulent Viking past. And, after they had come over in the ferry, she had quickly found a relatively inexpensive though tasteful bed-and-breakfast-style little hotel several miles from the nearest town, which was, anyway, the only town on the little island.

Most of their days were spent sitting in the garden and relaxing. He had his pipe, the only sin allowed him by Mrs. Huntingdon. She had him. There was just the two of them and therefore nothing new to talk about though Mrs. Huntingdon rehearsed her part in previous conversations while Mr. Huntingdon, pipe in mouth, nodded on and off. Usually off. Sometimes through his doze and beneath Mrs. Huntingdon's soliloquy he would catch strains of delightfully soporific music drifting from the living room of the little hotel.

Occasionally Mrs. Spence, the owner of the little hotel, would tiptoe into the garden to see if everything was fine and dandy with her guests. 'Is everything fine and dandy?' she would say. And if it was (and it usually was), Mrs. Huntingdon would tell her so.

If he were allowed to, Mr. Huntingdon would praise Mrs. Spence's lupins, a sweet-smelling mirage of brilliant colour. And Mrs. Spence would smile sweetly and leave the couple with the information that there would be a cup of tea for them at three if they so desired it. Mrs. Huntingdon affirmed that they would.

Mr. Huntingdon was a stonemason to trade and had built up a prosperous business through dedication and hard work. Among the sweat of the hard work and the worry of making ends meet adequately Mr. Huntingdon had sometimes resented his wife's effortless air of superiority. She was the daughter of a gentleman and was accustomed to gentility and exquisite sandwich spreads in delightful suroundings on summery afternoons. The fact that Mr. Huntingdon worked hard to provide her with an exact facsimile of her often-expressed expectations did not entirely satisfy her. And she said so. He, after all, worked with his hands, which was a bit common. He cut stone and obeyed architectural instructions from on high. He was a bit soiled, a bit crude, and very fortunate to have such a wife. She told him this often, and clearly implied that she was more than a cut above him. He accepted it openly and she never dreamed that he might resent being told it.

Nevertheless it was, on the face of it, a happy marriage. By working very hard and very long hours, Mr. Huntingdon had accumulated enough cash to buy himself into a firm and then, later (much later), to buy his partner out. He was now the owner of Huntingdon Constructions, his own boss, and possessor of a rather splendid specially built house — though Mrs. Huntingdon thought their home a bit common, too new to have genuine class.   There had been no children, because Mrs. Huntingdon did not, she said, want to be burdened by children.   And, to be fair, she had let him know this from the outset.   Apart from that, it was a happy marriage.   On the face of it.   Those who knew them said so.

After two weeks splendid isolation in their little hotel on the little island, Mrs. Huntingdon expressed a desire to see something.   He found plenty to look at around him: Mrs. Spence's lupins, the seductively curved and deep blue hills in the distance, the low clouds in the sky.   She, however, announced that they needed a change, a day out.   They would visit a tourist spot.   Not a common one, of course.   But it would be nice to see something.   Mr. Huntingdon would rather have stayed put, to let the quietness wash the dust out of his consciousness, but he was persuaded otherwise and quietly acquiesced.   She warned him it would appear uttterly common, completely philistine, to return from the little island without having been to one tourist attraction.   They would be showing her age.

So Mrs. Huntingdon bought a tourist book on the little island and selected, from a mass of data, the earth-house at Crabwick Farm.   This fitted her bill — it was not famous and would not therefore be the object of common admiration — and it would become the instrument of their outing.   She was certainly not going to mingle with the common tourists on their snap visits to obligatory attractions.   Their trip would be both edifying and exclusive.   They would be the only likely visitors to the earth-house on Crabwick Farm.

Mr. Huntingdon got the car ready and, at his wife's insistence, packed an extra can of petrol in the back because, as she said, there were hardly any petrol stations on the island, and she was not going to be stuck and stranded like a whale miles from civilisation.   Mr. Huntingdon then had to clean the car lest it had gathered dust while they had relaxed.   Then he had to find the earth-house despite the benefit of Mrs. Huntingdon's erratic front-seat navigation.   He did, eventually, find it.   And when he did, Mrs. Huntingdon said there was nothing there, nothing to be seen, until he convinced her that earth-houses were usually under the earth and that they would have to descend into it.

She decided to descend first and did so, after Mr. Huntingdon had lifted the iron grille up for her.   And when she was down he suddenly remembered he had left his comforting pipe and matches in the car and said he would be a second while he went for them.   'Just a second, mind,' she said from below.   'Just a second' was his incomplete echo.   And he hurried back to the car where he noticed, lying on the petrol can, the guide book to the little island.   The guide book he had not yet had the chance to read.   And he opened it at the section dealing with the earth-house.   And he began to read it at the part beginning: 'It is impossible to assert with total certainty the purpose or even the date or indeed the constructive principle............'

It is impossible to assert with total certainty the purpose or even the date or indeed the constructive principle behind the insular earth-houses.   In contra-distinction to the chambered and stalled cairns of the island, which are evidently truly megalithic conceptions, the earth-houses seem altogether more humble in origin, and were perhaps domestic devices rather than sacred places for the deposition of exalted human remains.   They are impossible to detect from a distance – again unlike the chambered cairns whose pregnant swelling mounds proudly proclaim a noble resting place – and were probably thought by their users to combine the maximum of secrecy with the minimum of discomfort.

Unlike the earth-houses discovered in the south, the insular examples give no indication of their antiquity. There are no relevant geological clues, no architectural anomalies, no runic inscriptions. While the general consensus of scholarly opinion is that the earth-houses belong to the bronze age, neolithic connexions cannot be entirely ruled out. It is also possible that, while southerners progressed beyond the common earth-house structure, the examples on the island testify to an indigenous anachronism.

Unique among the insular earth-houses is the example on Crabwick Farm, now deserted. The earth-house was discovered in 1920 by a passing ploughman whose heavy agricultural implement inadvertently penetrated the roof of the earth-house. It was excavated shortly afterwards under the direction of Dr. Martin Dramness, the archeologist who has since settled on the island, where he has built up an enviable reputation as the world's leading authority on insular earth-houses.

All earth-houses are constructed around a central chamber whose slabbed roof is supported by short monolithic pillars. The chamber is then reached by a short subterranean passageway. In the case of the Crabwick earth-house, the entrance tunnel was packed with loose earth which was filled with an astonishing profusion of limpet shells and razor shells. The chambered living room was uncontaminated by this earth, but the floor was littered with human remains: skulls and bones placed in a discernible pattern the significance of which has not yet been convincingly explained. In all, there were skeletal remains of five adults and fifteen children, and, as it is a tenet of scholarly faith that the earth-houses were not tombs, these must remain an enigmatic presence, an enduring mystery.

Today the visitor enters the chamber directly from an iron grating above. Once inside, he can see the entrance tunnel before him and the sandstone alcoves around him. To modern eyes it might seem inconceivable that more than three people could bear to huddle in such a confined space, but in times of storm and tempest and ever imminent attack, they must have afforded welcome shelter. The Crabwick earth-house is some four miles from the nearest road, though it is possible for a car to drive over a rough track to within two hundred yards of the Earth-house.

WEST ISLAND FREE PRESS

MYSTERY AT CRABWICK FARM

In one of the most macabre mysteries to hit this island for centuries the charred remains of a woman's body were found yesterday inside an ancient monument on a deserted farm (writes James Hardwick). Crabwick Farm, a deserted wasteland miles from a motor road, was the scene of a ghastly incident or appalling accident—and at the moment the local police cannot say which and are keeping an open mind on the subject. What is certain is that somehow some poor woman got trapped inside the neolithic earth-house on the farm and that somehow she became involved in a sudden blaze. When asked if petrol traces were found the police would not comment.

This is not, ironically, the first tragedy connected with Crabwick Farm and its ancient earth-house. Today it is visited infrequently by visitors or passing professors of archeology. It is completely concealed under the earth and is entered through an iron grating. There is no custodian, and the visitor is expected to enter and leave the earth-house as he or she found it. In this case the earth-house, built with flagstones supported by sturdy stone pillars, was undamaged but more serious is the air of tragedy that hangs around the earth-house.

The Crabwick earth-house was discovered years ago when a farm-worker smashed through part of the ancient roof. When the site was examined it was found that several skeletons lay inside. Who these skeletons had been and what they were doing there is to this day a mystery. Now the earth-house has claimed another victim and the public must ask: who was the woman and how did she come to be trapped in an ancient monument? The last person known to visit the earth-house was the local historian, Dr. Martin Dramness, and his visit was some two months ago.

It was Dr. Dramness, in search of material for the latest edition of his archeological survey of the island, who found the charred corpse. Asked if the tragedy could be connected to the bodies originally found in the earth-house, Dr. Dramness said there could be no connection whatsoever. However, he added: "Although we can only speculate as to the reasons for the presence of human remains found in the original excavations there is no, repeat no, way they could possibly connect with this appalling tragedy. This body I found is a modern remain, whereas the skeletal relics date from the time the earth-house was in domestic use, or so I am prepared to conjecture. It is regrettable that this should have happened—both for the sake of the dead woman and for the unfortunate connotations this may give to the earth-house in the popular imagination."

So far the Police have found no clues and are saying nothing. It looks as if the earth-house will keep its latest macabre secret — one, ironically, that is bound to revive flagging tourist attraction in the earth-house on Crabwick Farm.

THE VANDALS

THE VANDALS

Several decades after the crucifixion of Jesus Christ, the Romans —under the Governorship of Gnaeus Julius Agricola — penetrated Pictland as far north as the settlement of Marshend. In an attempt to subdue and pacify the local inhabitants, the Romans cut seven terraces into the hillside that dominated Marshend so the soldiers could command the territory they had conquered. When Agricola was recalled to Rome the Imperial presence in Marshend came to an end. The soldiers departed and the people swarmed back to the place. Marshend Hill remained, though, to stand over the village, and another conqueror, Edward I, noted it during his punitive expeditions north, when he hoped to reduce the countryside to a state unfit for human habitation. Today the seven Roman terraces are a spectacular feature of Marshend Hill, part of the tourist trap. Visitors can follow peacefully in the footsteps of the Roman soldiers.

Nineteen hundred years after Agricola's appointment to the Governorship of Britain, Gordon Miller came to stay in Marshend. He bought a little cottage in the shadow of Marshend Hill. He loved to watch the sun rising over the hill in the mornings. He didn't have much to do and especially liked to walk on the Roman terraces. He was elderly and alone and much given to daydreaming. Because he did not mix easily with the local people he was an object of curiosity. He was also extremely vulnerable. The first notice he had of his vulnerabality came one day after his usual walk on the terraces. He had wandered, as was his habit, from the bottom terrace to the top one and could see his cottage clearly from the summit of Marshend Hill. What he saw disturbed him. A group of youths hovered around his cottage door. There was something of a commotion. Then he heard the sound of glass breaking.

Being elderly, Gordon Miller had to take his time making the descent from the summit of the hill. When he reached the bottom he walked, as quickly as he could, to the cottage. Then he saw that his worst fears had been dramatically confirmed. The glass part of his front door — a large pane of pebbled glass — had been smashed. When he opened the door he saw a big stone on the floor surrounded by shattered fragments of glass. He was saddened, more than stunned. He could see no point whatever in the act. He had, as far as he could remember, done harm to nobody. He just wanted to be left in peace. Now his peace had been destroyed. There was little he could do about it.

Rather than reporting the incident to the local police and making himself conspicuous, Gordon Miller decided he would keep calm about the whole affair. It was after all, he reasoned, unlikely to happen again. He went to see the local joiner and had the damage repaired. It cost him more than he could easily afford from his pension, as his requirements were strictly budgeted. However, he felt he would have to accept the cost of the unfortunate incident philosophically.

Exactly a week later the new glass was broken.   Again a stone was thrown through it when Gordon Miller was on one of his walks.   This time he did report the incident to the police.   All two of them.   The two uniformed men came round to his cottage and inspected the damage.   They shook their heads and looked gravely around the house.   They then explained patiently — like indifferent adults explaining the facts of life to a backward child — that unless he could identify the culprits there was nothing they could do.   They advised him to take greater care of his property.   Then they left.

As he had always been a law-abiding citizen, Gordon Miller took notice of what the police said.   He stopped going out on his walks and instead stayed in and watched for intruders.   There was no sign of any menace for weeks, though occasionally couples walked hand in hand past the cottage on their way to the amorous privacy of the woods.   Gordon Miller's patience was rewarded eventually.   At least he had the opportunity to confront his tormentors.   One evening he decided to go to his bed exceptionally early and his pleasant dream was rudely interrupted by the sound of a crash.   Gordon Miller got up slowly and put the lights, and his dressing gown, on.   As he had guessed, the glass was smashed again and when he looked out there was nobody to be seen.   After about ten minutes, though, he heard footsteps and went to the door again.   Outside he could see, in the dusky light, six figures.   One of them stood in front of the other five.   They were grinning inanely.   Gordon Miller realised they were the enemy.

'Why are you doing this to me?' Gordon Miller asked wretchedly.

'Fuck off, ya auld goat!' the spokesman replied with a sneer.

Gordon Miller repeated his question.

The same young man gave the same answer.

Clearly this was a dead end.

'Why do you dislike me?' Gordon Miller asked, changing his approach.

'Ya fuckin heid case!' the young man observed by way of a riposte.

There was no answer from Gordon Miller.   The group then turned away and walked into the village.   Gordon Miller was left with a broken window and, it should be said, something of a broken heart.   He could not cope with this callous treatment.   He was sorry for himself.   He could see no point in any of it.   He wanted an explanation and had been given abuse.

Gordon Miller's mental stability had been based on the willingness of other people to reflect back the opinion he had of himself.   He saw himself as a respectable man who had carved out a respectable career in the Civil Service.   He had been in partial control of a department in which there were several young men and women under him.   They had always treated him with the utmost courtesy.   He had never had cause to dislike the young.   Instead he regarded himself as an avuncular presence who could reassure them.   When he had retired, the young men and women he worked with had presented him with a gold-plated watch.   Now this watch lay unwound on the mantelpiece in his cottage.   Time had ceased to have any crucial meaning for him.   It was no longer an important dimension.   He simply existed and waited for the next assault on his peace of mind.   He realised he was running out of goodwill.

His confrontations with the local gang were always the same.   He had become a figure of inexhaustible fun for them.   He could always be relied on to come out of his house and attempt to reason with them.   They always treated his ridiculous overtures the same way.   They ridiculed him, made him feel helpless and afraid.   Slowly his sense of self-respect was destroyed.   When, for the umpteenth time, his door-window was smashed he left it that way.   Instead of going to the joiners he walked down to a special shop the next morning and made a very special purchase.   When the shop-assistant asked him if he planned a bit of sport he ignored the question.   He walked home, aware of being looked at, with his long thin paper-covered acquisition.

It was early evening. The full moon was out and cast reflected light over the hillside. The terraces were dramatic in the moonlight. The youths who gathered outside Gordon Miller's cottage could see him on the summit of the hill, on the top terrace. He made a strange silhouette. One of the youths noticed he had something different with him. Something under his arm. The others sniggered collectively. Then the leading light of the group took his stone and threw it into the house as there was a gaping hole where the usual glass should have been. It wasn't quite so much fun, but they could always improvise new forms of entertainment at Gordon Miller's expense. 'Let's smash his other windaes!' the spokesman suggested. This was no sooner said than put into action. The six youths scooped up handfuls of gravel from the pathway to the cottage. Then they began to throw them at the front windows. In their ecstasy they were unaware of the approach of Gordon Miller.

Through the sound of the stones bouncing off the windows the unsteady voice of Gordon Miller came to the young men.

'Look here,' Gordon Miller said hopelessly.

The youths turned to face him.

'Christ allfuckinmighty!' one of them shrieked.

Gordon Miller held a double-barrelled shotgun in his hands and he was pointing it at them.

'Ye woudnae dae that you stupit auld bastart', the spokesman screamed.

One of his followers was not so sure. 'Fire that,' he said, 'and we'll kick yer fuckin heid in.'

That made Gordon Miller's decision much easier. The way he saw it he didn't actually have a choice. He raised the gun so the spread of shots would include them all. Then he fired.

Gordon Miller ended his days in the local asylum. He was a model patient. The staff liked him. He caused no problems for them and was quiet and introspective. He smiled a lot, mainly to himself, being rather uncommunicative. His one eccentricity was his obsession. He loved to play with his set of old lead Roman soldiers.

THE FERRET

With only an occasional excursion to the world outside it, Grant had spent his entire life in Marshend, a small Scottish whisky-distilling village. As the village had the economic blessing of full employment — Grant's parents worked, as did most of the other villagers, in the distillery — it was a peaceful place and proud of its quiet. There was a good turnout for the kirk on Sundays and local events were what really mattered. Neither the Scottish nor the English capitals held much interest for the inhabitants of Marshend; unlike provincial urban areas where the natives continually bear to the big cities as if magnetically attracted to a precious metal (and usually return with leaden steps), Marshend was self-sufficient, and a good place to grow up in.

For Grant, childhood had been one long game. There was an extensive wooded estate in and around the village, and the kids played there, climbing gigantic pine trees and guddling for the small trout that darted about in the little burn that twisted through the estate. At home, Grant had no feeling of insecurity, and the atmosphere in the village itself was soporofic. Grant and his pals simply passed the time of their young lives in delectable surroundings having fun.

Primary school was a laugh; secondary school was a riot. At primary school Grant and his pals did as little work as possible yet did not offend the teaching staff. After all, it was a local school. Secondary school was different, a big new building set in the nearest big town to which the village kids had to be brought by bus. It was at the town school that the Marshend kids became aware that the town folk regarded them as backward and even comical. This produced a positive reaction among the Marshend kids, and they formed a gang so they could clutch onto something familiar. The Marshend Maniacs — as the gang was called — was as numerous as any other in the school and much more cohesive. It was defensive rather than offensive, and to Grant it was exciting. He stopped going to kirk on Sundays and took upon himself the role of keeper of the conscience of the Marshend Maniacs.

There was nothing vicious about the Marshend gang. Never having been exposed to squalor or hardship they had not grown up with hate in their hearts. They could fight when they had to, but such fighting was in the nature of a 'square go': fist against fist, not boot and blade against fallen face. Grant and the other members of the gang got up to no advanced mischief and achieved local notoriety for their tremendous nuisance value. Still, they were local lads and tolerated in the village.

Grant was the most talkative member of the gang. It was he who became expert at setting up cheek to older folk and he got singled out as the leader of the pack, the motivating factor behind all the nonsense. A bad influence. He looked the part, too, with his bright blue eyes, his reddish fair hair, and his wide, cheeky grin. He loved to walk about the village with a pronounced swagger, conscious that he was being watched, was definitely somebody. More and more that mattered to Grant. Though the other members of the gang held back from serious trouble, Grant wanted thrills, and urged them to break the odd window. To the other members of the gang the whole thing was a joke, a phase: soon work would call them from school and jokes, and there would be responsibility and money and the steady preparation for married life. Grant dreaded this acceptance of the inevitable.

When they left school the Marshend Maniacs naturally applied for jobs at the distillery. There were always jobs at the distillery. It employed all types, from brilliant scientific researchers (to purify the product) to those who tidied up after the others. Most people fitted in between the two extremes but as Grant had elected to leave school without any qualifications whatever, he was obliged to accept cleaning work or nothing. He might have been better with nothing, for from the first day he started he realised he was no longer a somebody in the village: he was absolutely nobody in the distillery and everybody let him know it. Many of those he had teased and taunted were now in a position to order him about and they wanted him under the thumb. They aimed to get their own back.

'See what an idiot you've been,' Grant's immediate boss would say. 'You were told by your folks to stick in at school, but no, you knew best, and look where it's got you — sweeping the floors. Your father's done well here and your mother's a good worker, but you've let them down. You'll sweep up after others for the rest of your life. Every day you'll come in here and sweep up after your betters. That's where all your nonsense has got you. You'll be laughing on the other side of your face now.'

At first Grant turned the other cheek to this but after two weeks of it he had had enough. 'You can stick your job,' he told his boss. 'Who needs it? Who'd want to work in a dump like this?' And to prove his point he picked up a bottle of whisky and threw it against the wall: it shattered, and its familiar odour escaped into the air. The cost of that gesture was stopped out of Grant's wages. Now he was isolated in Marshend without a job and with a reputation for troublemaking. He knew he would find further local employment difficult: for one thing the distillery was *the* local employer; for another, word soon got around.

Far from being ashamed of his impulsive action, Grant was proud of what he had done. It got him talked about again and when he went into the pubs (the villagers get down to the serious business of drinking early in life) he was the main subject of conversation for a little while. 'Is it true you threw a bottle of their own whisky at the wall?' he would be asked. And he would incorporate in his answer fantastic variations on the actual event until he seemed like David facing Goliath. The whisky-throwing incident became infamous and Grant became good for a laugh in the pub. 'Have a drink on me, lad,' he would be told. 'You'll be short of a few bob just now.'

It soon dawned on Grant that if he did something bizarre in the village he would be noticed, while if he simply did an honest day's work nobody showed any interest in him. From people who sympathised with his parents or who remembered the carefree young boy he had been —from them Grant got a few jobs. But he repaid the helpful gestures with contemptuous clowning and kept getting fired. He was sacked from the local ironmongers for swearing at the boss; sacked from a paper mill for throwing huge paper aeroplanes at other employees; sacked from a pub in an adjoining village for attempting to drink the stock. Thereafter unemployment.

The former members of the now defunct Marshend Maniacs ceased to take an interest in Grant. They had steady jobs and began to find Grant's conversation tiresome. He was drinking excessively now, knocking back as much as he could afford, and in his cups he would make the wildest suggestions, like kidnapping someone and hiding them in a cellar and demanding ransom. Or robbing a bank. His friends would humour him for a while and end up telling him to get a job. 'Think of your parents,' they would say. They of all people! For Grant this was the ultimate treason. He had gone out of his way to entertain his friends since childhood — and had done so by virtue of his irresponsibility, which they had encouraged by their appreciative laughter. Now they wanted to drop him and get on with their boring jobs and boring girlfriends. And they wanted Grant to get on with his parents, when, in fact, life at home was unbearable now with his father accusing him of alchoholism and his mother implying insanity. He had to shut himself in his bedroom downstairs in the house while they watched telly upstairs. Then he would turn up the volume on his radio and drown out their presence with pop music.

Still, there was one person in Marshend who would pass the time of day with Grant, and this was Jimmy, the local poacher, a man in his sixties. Nobody bothered about Jimmy being a poacher for he didn't harm anybody. He would roam the estate seeking clusters of rabbit holes. Then he would put his snares over selected holes and ram his ferret into another hole. When the ferret-tormented rabbits came thundering out into the snares Jimmy would kill them with a quick Karate-chop to the neck. Later he would sell them locally or in nearby villages. He was as brown as a berry and as cunning as a fox, was old Jimmy.

Grant took to going out with Jimmy and watching him ferret. He made a good and useful companion and would run any errands the old man wanted. He asked for no reward but old Jimmy gave him one: a ferret of his own. A lively, inquisitive ferret that clung to Grant when it wasn't being sent to seek out rabbits. Grant loved to send the beast scurrying down dark narrow holes in search of rabbits. His ferret was a good one and he began to carry it about with him in an old canvas schoolbag, inked with slogans from the days of the Marshend Maniacs. With his ferret he felt important, for it provoked comment when its head burst out of the corner of the bag and put the fear of death into those who thought they smelled a rat. Grant would laugh at their fear, but soon the novelty wore off. Grant got restless again.

One night old Jimmy came into the local pub and was astonished by what he saw. Grant was, as usual, in the wee room at the back. He was sitting at a table with a wide grin on his face, several glasses in front of him, and he was clearly very very drunk indeed. He was alone, save for the presence on the jukebox of his ferret. The animal just lay dead still on the jukebox though the machine was pounding out loud raucous pop music. 'You're drunk, lad,' Jimmy rasped impatiently. 'Aye, and so's the ferret,' Grant laughed. 'I got it drunk. I gave it twa pints o' slack and it really lapped it up, lapped it up, had its wee nose right down into the glass when I tipped it over.'   It was obvious to old Jimmy that the little animal was indeed drunk, for its natural vitality had been obliterated by the relatively huge amount of alchohol it had consumed.   'You're a bigger bloody fool than I thought, lad,' Jimmy said as he walked out of the bar.   Grant was so much under the weather that he did not realise he had forfeited the sympathy of old Jimmy.   He simply turned and smiled at the incapacitated ferret and offered his pint glass to the sleeping animal.

But that was not the end of Grant's story.   The day after he had got drunk with his ferret in the wee room at the back of the local, the police came to see him.   After hammering on the door they managed to wake him — it was early, but his father and mother were already away to work.   It seemed that a sheep had been stolen from the estate: shot, stolen and hidden in the empty pigsty at the back of old Jimmy's house.   Jimmy's relatives in a nearby village confirmed that the old man had been with them all day, so somebody had hidden the sheep in his pigsty and the police reckoned that that somebody was Grant. Grant's first reaction was to laugh at the policemen.   The story sounded so funny, somebody stealing a sheep and hiding it in a pigsty.   To him it sounded like the sort of thing old Jimmy would do.   But, as the police told him, Jimmy couldn't have done it, whereas Grant was known to hang around the estate, was known to the police, was the sort of lad who was always up to no good.   He was going to be charged.

Grant pleaded not guilty in court, but nobody believed in his innocence any more.   For this crime — and the court contended it was a crime — he was heavily fined, though, as he was not working, it meant that the cash would have to be deducted from his unemployment money.   He was ostracised in Marshend for his court appearance. Folk passing in the street would hiss epithets like *'despicable'*, *'disgusting'*, *'criminal'*.   He was not even acceptable in the pubs in the village.   Most of all, his old mates ignored him.   His parents, though appalled, did not throw him out immediately but gave him one week in which to find a place of his own — the further from Marshend the better.

Thus on the Monday he lay in his bedroom listening to the radio with some bottles of cheap wine beside the bed and his ferret on the bed. It was a warm night and the window of the bedroom was open. Grant was depressed, but had drunk himself into a state of devil-may-care weariness. He gave some wine to the ferret, and when the animal gladly took it, he offered it some more. He was amused, rather than amazed, to see the ferret sup up the wine and saw that soon it was hopelessly drunk. He laughed as he put it on top of the radio so the sounds of pop music beat into its furry body. The animal made no movement but lay there flaked out. Grant giggled.

When he decided to get some sleep he had a last look at the ferret, lying there drunk on top of the still pulsating radio. It was relatively lucky he thought, it did not have to look for a place to live in. When the light went out, Grant's consciousness soon followed it, for the wine had taken toll of his troubles. He lay there and soon his mouth sagged open and he began to snore. That, and the cold breeze that suddenly swept in through the open window, seemed to waken the ferret on the radio. It looked around the room and, suddenly feeling lively again, made for the window and the world beyond it. It sneaked off to its dark liberty. In its absence Grant continued to snore and the radio kept on its incessant beat while upstairs Grant's parents fretted over the future of their son.

A SCOTTISH ZHIVAGO

A SCOTTISH ZHIVAGO

Edinburgh may seem a long way from Russia — or even Spain where the movie was made —but it was watching *Doctor Zhivago* on television that reminded me of an evening in my native city in the mid-sixties when David Lean's film first appeared in the cinemas.   It was a summer evening and Sunday drinking was still something of an event in Scotland.   Only the hotels were open for service and I was sitting at home minding my business when John, a friend, dropped in to see if I was going out.   For a drink, of course; that was the only thing to tempt the sober (as opposed to the church-going) citizen out on the Sabbath.   So out we went.

I then lived in a flat in a square at the top of Leith Walk and we strolled across the garden and headed for the long curving terrace on the more favoured side of the Walk.   We went up to a classy-looking hotel, gravitated towards the bar and ordered our drinks.   Nothing exotic; just the usual pints of heavy.

In the corner of the bar a man sat playing an accordion.   It made a change from the usual juke box, being more human, and it was cheaper, too, for the man wanted nothing but a few kind words and a drink from time to time.   He played what the customers wanted, and John immediately put in a request for *Lara's Theme* from *Doctor Zhivago*.   The accordionist was happy to oblige.

'That's our song,' said John, whose instant ability to coin a cliche was an oddly acceptable part of his personality.

'Who's us?' I asked him.

'Me and Linda.'

Now I had seen John out with Linda on a couple of occasions but had no idea he was so enthusiastic about what looked like a casual affair. But as the minutes dissolved into hours and the pints became gallons, I realised that John was absolutely serious. He was, he assured me, devoted to Linda. He loved her with an intensity that was overwhelmimg. He saw the film of *Doctor Zhivago* as a glorious work of art that related to the romance between himself and Linda. He, of course, was Zhivago; or, rather, Omar Sharif. Linda was Lara (or Julie Christie). To John it was as simple as that.

Looking at him in the quiet glow and relaxed atmosphere of the hotel bar I could see a faint resemblance between John and Omar Sharif. The hang-dog eyes were similar, the colour of the hair corresponded. Sharif, though, was what passed as handsome in the outside world. John's was a typically Scottish face. He had the expansive area between upper lip and nostrils, the eyebrows coming together in an inverted 'V', and a boozy complexion. He was heading fast for premature middle-aged Scottishness. Not so Omar Sharif.

I tried to recall Linda's face. Plump, I'd have called her. She was certainly more massive than Julie Christie, yet both women were fair of hair and complexion. Linda was not stunningly goodlooking the way Julie Christie was in the film though John had convinced himself she was. The connexion between the screen and the reality was a figment of John's imagination —which was not a bad thing. It was good to have a vivid imagination and to have aspirations. Sharif and Christie were the Platonic ideals of which John and Linda were imperfect earthly copies.

By the time drinking-up time came round — which always meant a rush for last orders and a chat with the manager to obtain a surreptitious carry-out of drink — John was well gone and maudlin. He'd had *Lara's Theme* played at least a dozen times and told everyone in the bar about his love for Linda. He was patted on the back, he was congratulated, he was told how happy he would be when he married her. For that was John's intention. He would marry Linda and take her away to another country — a land more lovely than Scotland, a place fit for her matchless character. He was very drunk indeed.

As we left the hotel we stood and looked at Edinburgh's spectacular skyline and its faint gleam of hope. It was Scott's own romantic town but it was also John's city of romance. It felt good to be close to a dreamer who believed in his dreams. While we were standing there, transported, a couple came close and I recognised the large female shape as Linda. I'd been thinking about her face quite a bit that night, so I knew it was her. I elbowed John but he had already seen. She walked past with a wave.

'Hello, John. Hi.'

That was all she said. She looked like a young lady who had no idea of the emotional heat generated on her behalf that evening. John said nothing. He gaped open-mouthed at this parade of grim reality on a Scottish Sunday. Later, when he recovered (as well as he could), he told me he was finished with Linda, that that was the end of that, that he'd never trust women again. He told me, as we consumed the carry-out in my flat, that he'd go through with his plan to leave Scotland anyway. He hated the country and the people. Everything made him miserable. He would strike out on his own.

'I'll probably take off for Australia,' he told me.

'Sounds promising,' I agreed.

John never did go to Australia, but he did get married. Not to Linda, though. I heard she married the Frenchmen she was with the night she passed by. She then went to live in Paris. John learned to live with it. He became less of a dreamer, more of a cynic. He grew visibly older and sadder as he settled down to spend his days and what was left of his youth in Edinburgh. Whether he was wiser as a result of the experience I do not know for he certainly never mentioned Linda again. Not to me anyway.

THE PYGMALION PILL

Struthers-Brown had the kind of voice that could silence his staff with a well-chosen syllable. With an expensively exclusive public school education behind him, he felt that the most effective weapon in the class war was the colour of one's moneyed accent. As Struthers-Brown saw it, the mass of people, however much they might resent the fact, had been conditioned for generations to respond deferentially to the upper-crust voice. All he had to do was open his mouth and lesser beings cringed before vocal sounds that seemed to have the majesty of a mighty Empire behind them. A chap with a voice like that just *had* to be right and decent and respectable and all things bright and, damn it, beautiful.

At school Struthers-Brown had been rather poor academically but that did not matter. With total self-confidence he would bring to any subject in a school debate his expansive assurance. Although his brighter fellow scholars might mock the empty platitudes emerging from just below Struthers-Brown's stiff upper lip, he remained unperturbed. He simply continued to trot out his simple version of official Victorian morality and described his opponents as bounders. Basically, Struthers-Brown's philosophy of life could be summed up in his favourite phrase: *'the country's not what it was'* — well, he would see that the tenets of a glorious past governed his firm's future.

Struthers-Brown was much too young to know much about his country's past and his performance at history at his expensive school did not qualify him as a serious authority on the good old gone days. Yet Struthers-Brown had his confidence. He instinctively knew the difference between right and wrong. His father, who had recently died, was the source of his opinions — his father and, just possibly, the school chaplain. Struthers-Brown senior had been a military gent of some distinction somewhere, and, despairing of the way the country was going, had determined to mould his son into the model of the true Englishman. For Struthers-Brown there was God, and, next to God, the Monarch. That was really all there was to know.

As he entered middle-age, Struthers-Brown could feel pretty proud of himself. He was managing director of a firm specialising in unusual inventions with a patriotic flavour. A firm that catered, so Struthers-Brown liked to think, for the Englishman's individuality. For example, they supplied their customers — a very exclusive set — with iced-water bottles, with shotguns that when fired played '*Land Of Hope And Glory*', with burglar alarms that when set off produced an authoritarian voice that screamed '*By God, I'll deal with you good and proper when I catch you, you bounder.*' That kind of thing.

Some of the items were incredibly ingenious and so Struthers-Brown had to deal with scientists, people he thought of as uncommonly common, ostentatiously vulgar. But he tolerated them because they helped to make a profit for the firm, and if the firm was making a profit, so Struthers-Brown believed, it was doing a damn good job for England. No man could ask for more. Struthers-Brown himself had no grasp whatsoever of scientific principles — nor wanted to grasp such things. He saw himself as the element that guaranteed the firm's high standing. Some of the firm's items might have a touch of levity, but they were never vulgar. Struthers-Brown saw to that.

He had literally walked into the job. At the interview he asserted himself with his resounding upper-class accent, paraded his family connexions with the board of directors, and got the managing directorship. Yes, he felt a happy contented man, one of the bulldog breed moiling and toiling and doing his best for his country.

Monday morning was his favourite morning. Struthers-Brown did not smoke and did not drink — to excess — and usually spent Sundays riding round the estate he had inherited from his father. Unlike Struthers-Brown, many of his employees would come in of a Monday morning clearly the worse for wear, several of them groaning under the obvious weight of a hangover.   It was then that Struthers-Brown, proud of his moral superiority to such reprobates, would approach them and assault their bruised consciousnesses with his hearty manner and massive voice.

'Good morning, good morning, Hawkins,' he would bark at some unfortunate, who usually happened to be Hawkins.   'How are you this wonderful morning, then?   Tell me, tell me what is your honest opinion of the company's cash inflow figures?   Would you, old chap, be inclined to give us a clean bill of fiscal health?   I take it you have perused the latest figures — the Chairman's statement as I don't need to tell you, was published in Saturday's *Financial Times*.   Come on now, Hawkins, we are constantly, are we not, hearing of the moral imperative of management and staff existing, as it were, in a state of symbiosis? Aren't we, Hawkins, aren't we?   Well then, Hawkins: I'm after your considered opinion.   I take it that you have cogitated sufficiently, and now I expect you to expatiate.'

At that poor old Hawkins — or whoever it happened to be of a breezy Monday morning (usually Hawkins) — would look down at the floor and shuffle uncomfortably and make a meaningless gesture. And that pleased Struthers-Brown.   It confirmed what he instinctively knew: that he was a superior breed to the men who worked for him.   He knew what was right and wrong whereas they knew nothing.   Give them a chance to speak and, damn it, they would look away.   No, Struthers-Brown told himself, that sort will never take over the world.   Not in a million years.

Struthers-Brown often tested the power of his presence over his staff in precisely this way, and he never failed to impress himself.   It was not, he was sure, the fact that he had the power of hire and fire over the people he talked to.   It was that they knew they were dealing with a man of quality.   A first class chap and no mistake.

The pathetic sight of Hawkins's pathetic humble diffident grovelling that Monday morning told Struthers-Brown he was still in command, still the monarch of all he surveyed on the shop floor.   On occasion, if he approached with stealth, he would hear Hawkins, or someone like him, passing uncouth opinions on the way the firm was run. The diatribe would run something like this: 'I mean, take Mr. Struthers-Brown, old God Almighty himself — he don't know nothing of conditions on the shop floor. I mean, the like of him's always had it easy — born with a silver spoon in his how's your father. I'd like to see him putting in an honest day's graft on the shop floor. No bleeding chance of that. If he had to make up some of the jobs we get — all complicated, like — he'd have a heart attack. Wouldn't know his how's your father from his elbow.'

At such a moment Struthers-Brown would suddenly emerge and say something suitably menacing like: 'Ah, Hawkins, just the man I want to see. Just the very chap to consult on the proposed streaming of the work force. Do you, and I ask you advisedly, Mr. Hawkins, have any constructive ideas about disposing of what we might metaphorically refer to as dead wood? Any succinct suggestions for a meaningful cutback in staff?' And of course Hawkins would shuffle and shrug and stare at the floor.

Struthers-Brown was of the opinion that his hereditary superiority to his staff was reflected in his physical advantages over them. Take Hawkins. Hawkins was a prematurely old forty-year-old, three years older than Struthers-Brown himself. He had all the appearance of a defeated man. His hair was thinning rapidly, his cheeks were grey and sunken, and his stooped posture was an emblem of his surrender. Struthers-Brown, on the other hand, was tall, upright, assured. He walked with his elbows well out to the side as if edging more room for himself with each second. His hair was still profuse though there was a distinguished dappling of grey at his temples. He looked every inch a managing director.

So that Monday morning he was in excellent fettle, ready to make decisions that would change the course of his profit margin. As he strutted into his office, his secretary, a charmingly attractive young lady without a hint of vulgarity, told him he had an appointment. He was to grant an audience to a gifted young scientist, a Dr. Graham Freer. Struthers-Brown acknowledged receipt of the information and settled himself at his desk, busying himself with blank sheets of paper.

At 10.30 there was a buzz on the intercom and Struthers-Brown's secretary announced the prompt arrival of Dr. Freer. Struthers-Brown indicated that the scientist be admitted. And it was accomplished. The door was opened and Struthers-Brown confronted what to his eyes looked like a very scruffy young man with an unkempt beard and excited rapid eye movements. The scientist had thick glasses — a sign of degeneracy in the opinion of Struthers-Brown — and he peered at Struthers-Brown and his eyes darted from side to side behind the thick lenses of his glasses.

'Yes?' enquired Struthers-Brown magisterially. Dr. Freer began to speak rapidly as if there was not a second to be wasted: 'I have made an incredible chemical discovery, a pill — I call it the Pygmalion Pill — based on a structural reduction of the compounds.....' but Struthers-Brown stopped the scientist's flow with a wave of his hand. 'I don't want the technical details,' he told Dr. Freer. 'Such things are competently dealt with by the staff I retain to look after such matters. Please confine your remarks to two things: first, the nature of your invention or discovery or whatever; second, the application of your invention or discovery or whatever. Care for a cigar?'

Non-smoker Struthers-Brown opened a large polished box containing large dull cigars. Dr. Freer declined the offer. He was determined to put his case without delay as he had been told by Struthers-Brown's secretary that her boss was an exceptionally busy man. 'Well, Mr. Struthers-Brown, the thing is this. I have discovered, developed, a pill that, up to a period of twenty-four hours, can radically alter the nature of the individual's speech patterns. It has both a physiological and psychological effect and the combined impact is to give anyone access to a chemically-induced perfect received pronunciation.'

'Received pronunciation,' Struthers-Brown demanded impatiently, 'What the devil are you talking about, man?'

'An accent like, well, like your own one. Think of what it could mean to the mass of people. By taking a pill in the morning, each morning — after shaving or brushing one's teeth — any citizen can possess a perfectly acceptable posh accent. An accent that hitherto only money could buy. Shopgirls could discourse to lady clients on terms of phonetic equality. There would be no class barriers on account of the contents of your mouth. Applicants for jobs would not be discriminated against because of their vowel-sounds. We have already done away with racial and sexual barriers. My pill will do away with conversational barriers. The common cockney will be equally presentable, vocally speaking, as the headmaster of a top public school. Every man will have a voice like yours.'

Struthers-Brown had taken enough of this. 'Do you realise what you are saying?' he asked the scientist. 'You are proposing some cockeyed plan to eliminate the moral fibre of our society. A voice like mine, as you impertinently call it, is the result of ethical and educational and financial and religious and hereditary and....and, well, every sort of proper inculcation.'

'Precisely,' the scientist added 'And now all this will be available by swallowing a tasteless pill.'

'Tasteless. Yes, now you are talking. Tasteless is the exact epithet I was searching for. It just about sums the whole damn silly business up. Tasteless. First, I don't believe in the existence of such a pill. Second, even if such a monstrous pill could be developed I know of no one who would be willing to market it. Third, the proper place for the acquisition of a proper accent is at home and at school. Fourth, you have taken up enough of my time. Good Morning.'

'But, Mr. Struthers-Brown,' persisted the scientist, 'you are turning down the chance to revolutionise society. At last there can be equality of opportunity because no one will know, from speech patterns, whether a man be a lord or a labourer.'

'Revolutionise!' Struthers-Brown reiterated ferociously. 'Revolutionise — yes, I should have known you were a damned rebel, a revolutionary. If I had my way I'd have the likes of you locked in the Tower. As it unfortunately happens, I can do no such thing. But mark my words, your little scheme to bolster the confidence of the lower orders — and that is all your plan is, a damned confidence trick — has not the slightest chance of getting anywhere. I will see to it that you will be denied access to the boardrooms of this country; I will ensure that your name — my secretary has a note of the wretched thing — is mud. And don't think, by the way, you can fool me. If you had such a thing as your damn pill why would you speak in such a seedy, sloppy way? You're not dealing with a fool, you know!'

Standing up, Dr. Freer played his last, his best, card. 'I anticipated this objection, Mr. Struthers-Brown, and if you will provide me with a glass of water I will demonstrate the effects of my pill — see, I have a supply with me. My voice will change, before your very eyes......'

But Struthers-Brown was already on the intercom. 'Miss Mathews, ask security to come and.....'

'All right,' said Dr. Freer, defeated by the threat of forced removal, 'I'll go.'

'Cancel that command,' Struthers-Brown told Miss Mathews through the intercom. 'The gentleman will be leaving now of his own accord.'

That was that. Dr. Freer left without another word. Struthers-Brown, not normally given to alcoholic indulgence, needed a strong drink to wash the taste of the interview out of his mouth. He had a nightmare vision of society destroyed by a confounded pill that would, at a stroke, knock down the barriers that society had taken centuries to erect. He asked Miss Mathews to bring him a glass and a bottle of whisky. He poured himself a large measure and, with trembling fingers, drank deeply of it.

The first thing Dr. Freer did when he came out of Struthers-Brown's office was to bump —literally — into Mr. Hawkins on his way up from the shop floor.   Dr. Freer apologised and was about to walk on when Mr.Hawkins, on a specific point of information, asked Dr. Freer in what kind of mood the managing director was.

'Well, I don't really know,' said Dr. Freer, 'because I haven't met the man before, but if rude, unreasonable, bad-tempered, malicious behaviour is his norm, then he is quite normal.'

'Like that, is it,' said Mr. Hawkins, already hesitant about approaching Struthers-Brown on the question of a request for an early holiday.   'Well, I'd better not bother him if he's going on like that.'

The shared distaste both men felt for Struthers-Brown brought them together and they began to talk about this and that.   Eventually Mr. Hawkins, who had decided to come to see his boss during the coffee break lest he be accused of time-wasting, invited Dr. Freer to come and have a cup of coffee with him in the canteen.   Naturally Dr. Freer, in the throes of disappointment and with nowhere to go, accepted, and even confided his secret to Mr. Hawkins.   Equally naturally, Mr. Hawkins expressed a keen interest in the apparently miraculous pill.   The Pygmalion Pill.   In fact, Mr. Hawkins offered to try it out on himself, there and then, and suggested he might wash it down with a second cup of coffee.

Now, as luck or misfortune would have it, that Monday morning was important for a special reason.   A small group of major shareholders had arranged to come round to inspect the factory, to see what kind of state prevailed at the source of their profits.   They had asked to see the impeccable Mr. Struthers-Brown at 3 p.m.   All the major shareholders — there were ten of them — had met Mr. Struthers-Brown before and had been impressed by his bearing, by his assurance, by his glib certainty.   They were, however, unprepared for the spectacle that awaited them when they arrived at Mr. Struthers-Brown's office at the appointed hour.

For Mr. Struthers-Brown had been drinking, and it was very

obvious to all he had been drinking. For one thing, he slurred his words most disgracefully, and there was an empty bottle of whisky and an empty glass on his desk. Miss Mathews, Struthers-Brown's secretary, had thought of advising her inebriated employer to call it a day, to stage a convenient illness, to go home and sleep it off. Yet she knew that Struthers-Brown had never taken a day off in his working life and she dared not face the consequences of offering such an exalted being such mundane advice.

Thus it was that the major shareholders were ushered into the office at 3 p.m., to see Struthers-Brown so obviously in his cups. Miss Mathews was painfully aware of his condition. The major shareholders were quickly aware of it. Only Struthers-Brown carried on as if nothing had happened. He was in no position to realise that his sibilants were slushy, that his vowels were wobbly.

'Sit down,' he murmured to the major shareholders. 'We'll all have a little drink before your conducted tour.' Unaware of the disapproving glances his condition provoked, Mr. Struthers-Brown requested from Miss Mathews another bottle of whisky plus ten glasses. He then proceeded to fill the glasses as well as he was able and gulped down a large whisky. Refreshed, he announced his breezy intention of taking the major shareholders round the firm. He clambered on his feet and tottered towards the door and left. Then the major shareholders left, leaving on the table ten untouched glasses of malt whisky.

Led by the unsteady, swaying, utterly ridiculous figure of Struthers-Brown, the ten major shareholders were taken round the factory. Where he had intended a march of triumph, Struthers-Brown only succeeded in disgracing himself in front of the ten major shareholders and, even worse, his staff. The staff sniggered to see such a thing — the great Struthers-Brown reeling like a street-corner drunk. It looked to all and sundry as if Struthers-Brown had quietly gone to pieces.

Gradually it dawned on Struthers-Brown that he was making an ass of himself, and he felt the only way he could redeem himself was by demonstrating to the ten major shareholders the degree of awe in which his staff held him. He thought of Hawkins. Hawkins had been conditioned, through innumerable Monday mornings, to instant humility, so Struthers-Brown made unsteadily for Mr. Hawkins. He was followed by the outraged ten major shareholders.

'Aha, Hawkins,' mumbled Struthers-Brown. 'And how are we this fine afternoon, old man, old bean, old son? Still up to the minute and the mark on how the old firm is progressing, what? Still my man in the know? Hawkins, let me introduce you to the senior shareholders. Perhaps you could give them a rundown on how things are on the shop floor?'

It took Mr. Hawkins a couple of seconds to discover the drift of Struthers-Brown's barely coherent questions. When he understood, he addressed himself to the ten major shareholders — and in an upper-crust voice. 'I'm overwhelmed that Mr. Struthers-Brown should have chosen me to say a few words to such important visitors. And I'm glad to say something about the nature of things on the shop floor. Basically, the problem in this firm is the lack of cooperation between top management — embodied in the person of Mr. Struthers-Brown — and the operatives on the shop floor. We produce the goods, in a very literal sense. We deal directly with the inventive scientific personnel and execute their imaginative insights to the best of our abilities. We translate their dreams into reality. We feel the top management has only the most schematic idea of the complex nature of our novelties, and are convinced we could increase profits if we had a more substantial say in the running of the firm. Provided, of course, that a percentage of the profits was ploughed back into research and that increased productivity would be rewarded by a sound bonus scheme.'

Struthers-Brown was astonished, horrified. 'Pull yourself together, Hawkins,' he spluttered. 'Talk in your normal voice. Behave as your normal stupid deferential self. Stop acting.'

'I beg your pardon, sir,' said Mr. Hawkins, with upper-crust assurance.

'You damn bounder, you snake in the grass, I'll dismiss you for this, I'll.....I'll....I'll.....' And, so saying, Mr. Struthers-Brown collapsed in a heap on the floor.

The major shareholders had seen enough. At an Extraordinary General Meeting, they reported on their visit to the factory and made two recommendations. First, that Mr. Hawkins be appointed managing director. Second, that Mr. Struthers-Brown be retained as entertainments officer.

And so it was that Mr. Hawkins became one of the most succesful managing directors in the country. And so it was that an obscure scientist, Dr. Graham Freer, became technical consultant to Mr. Hawkins. And so it was that the great Pygmalion Pill was launched on the open market with the dramatic social consequences we now accept as part of everyday life. As for Mr. Struthers-Brown—somewhere in the recesses of his fuddled consciousness there is a plan for the restoration of his good self to his former glory. For he studies tapes of the old common cockney accent, so that he might master it and have, once more, a unique voice in a unique firm.

THE FIRST POEM

The first time I saw Paris I was sixteen and still at school. I'd never been out of Edinburgh before and often ached to visit foreign places I'd seen in films. Of all the places I'd experienced vicariously, Paris was the most special. It had everything. Well, it had Brigitte Bardot for one thing, and that one thing was what most obsessed me at sixteen. I could never have afforded to go to Paris if it had not been for a chance meeting. A man who lived adjacent to the street where I lived had heard about me going back to school after a year away from it. I had left for good, with no qualifications whatsoever, and had ended up in a bakery. Impulsively, I had decided I didn't want to be a baker, really, so had applied to the school for re-entry, and, astonishingly, was accepted. That, though, is another story. This man, Mr. Macleod, was a retired banker with a timber business in Fife. He was unmarrried, childless and alone, and I suppose he wanted to do something worthwhile in his old age. What he decided to do was finance a trip to France for me.

It all happened so casually, this meeting with a genuine do-gooder. One day, on my way home from school, he beckoned me over and asked me if there were any subjects I was having difficulty with at school. I told him French. Later I would rationalise this difficulty and argue, with Bernard Shaw, that no man who is master of one language can master another. Then, I just found French difficult. And turgid. I hated having to stand up in class and ape the French accent with those sounds that came out like someone with a bad case of catarrh. He asked me if I'd like to go to France. I said Yes. He said he'd fix it. And he did. Just like that. My father was dead and my mother agreed to the visit. So at the tender age of sixteen I was presented with a ticket, a booking in a Parisian hotel, and more than enough money to carry me through the holiday. It was an extraordinary gesture on the part of Mr. Macleod; he's dead now but I'll always be grateful to him for what he did. The holiday was a seminal experience. It gave me a chance to meet Doris.

Paris in July washed over me like a great heatwave. It was festive and fun and there was scaffolding everywhere for Bastille Day on the 14th. It was a whole sensuous world away from dreich Edinburgh. I felt in my own element for the first time in my life. Edinburgh at that time was an oppressive presence; it represented defeat. I had been born there and nothing had really happened to me until my temporary escape to Paris. I knew Edinburgh was reality and that eventually I would have to return to face reality. For the moment there were the sights and sounds and scents (black coffee and French fags) of Paris.

On returning to school I had taken a fanatical interest in painting, inspired in that direction by my best pal Sandy Moffat (now recognised as an outstanding painter). I had gobbled up every fact about painting I could possibly digest and was ready to regurgitate the whole history of art (as I then saw it) at the drop of a *faux pas*. I was mad about the French painters. So much had happened in Paris and I was set to take it all in. I had decided I wasn't going to tell anybody I was a schoolkid, so I planned my holiday *persona* as a young art historian who had studied painting and could, you understand, knock off a painting if the desire came. It might happen after all: *sait-on jamais*.

A couple of days before Bastille Day it rained in Paris and I, fresh from the Louvre and a walk, rushed to take shelter under the scaffolding in the Place de la Concorde. When I looked at my fellow-shelterers I noticed a girl standing beside me. She was a knock-out. Fair hair, delicious features, superb body (what I could see of it): the lot. Having left my conscience behind in Edinburgh, I exploited my new confidence and introduced myself in French. She realised right away I was no Frog and answered in English. Then there was the business about explaining I was Scottish, not English. All that bullshit. I told her I was an art historian, also a painter, and she told me about herself. She was Swiss, her name was Doris, and she was a qualified physiotherapist who intended to have a look at London after Paris and then fly to the USA to take up a professional position in South Carolina. The drama of the situation — boy meets smasher in Paris — impressed itself on me, and I decided to make a play for her. She was clearly a wee bit older than me, perhaps twentyone. That didn't matter. I thought I'd bring a little light into my life and she was the highlight on a shining Paris. It had stopped raining, the wet glistened on the pavements. The Place de la Concorde was an island surrounded by a wet blur of motorcars. I had the girl of my dreams on my island. She started to walk and I walked with her. Halfway there.

I talked a lot about art and it was apparent she had a pretty thorough knowledge of post-cubist painting at least. That suited me. We walked a lot and when we paused at the UNESCO building I praised the mural by Joan Miro, pronouncing the prename like a Scottish lassies's name. Doris laughed, not cruelly, but she was highly amused. She told me the correct Spanish pronunciation of Joan Miro, and I felt like a right eedjit. I thought how sophisticated she was in comparison with me. I still had the Edinburgh street mentality and she was clever and witty and without any fakery. We made a fine pair: a contrast rather than a combination. It worked, though; that was all that mattered.

I must have amused Doris a lot that day because she laughed a lot. I remember we walked down Montmartre — inevitably — and there was a neon sign with an outline that looked to me like a pair of spectacles above the caption *Pour Ma Ligne.* Thinking I had reached the height of wit, I pointed at it and said, fatuously, 'Advertising for spectacles, eh, they're a bit shortsighted.' She laughed loudly, to my embarrassment, and told me that the text of the advertisment meant 'For My Figure' and that the illustration was a schematic depiction of a brassiere. I blushed; or, as we'd have said back home, I got a red neck. The super sophisticate from Scotland had blundered! Of course this made her seem all the more sexy to me, a female who could openly speak about things like that. Excitedly I gestured to a stripclub. She asked if I wanted to go in. 'No,' I told her, 'When I studied painting I used to do nude studies all the time, it's no novelty to me.' That bit of mendacity would, I hoped, restore her opinion of me. She suppressed a smile with a change of subject. She did not look entirely convinced by the Caledonian Courbet.

The day lingered on and dusk came down on Paris like a diaphanous mauve curtain. We were sitting by the Seine and she chatted pleasantly about her future in America. Great to have a future mapped out for you like that! Me, I was uncertain what life held in store for me, though I felt deeply sad at the thought of a Doris-less future. My mind was on the present and Paris and Doris, whose name chimed with Paris. I asked her about physiotherapy and she told me the little details of her job. Then I remembered I'd a sore wrist (a lie, of course) and asked her to treat it for me. She gently massaged my wrist and it was delightful to be touched by her. It was one thing necking a bird back on the Calton Hill; quite another dimension to be held by a Swiss girl in Paris by the Seine. I let her fingers linger on my wrist until she got up and announced it was time for her to return to her hotel. No, she didn't want me to walk her home, that wasn't necessary. Yes, she'd meet me by the river next morning. I almost skipped all the way back to my hotel. I had clicked with her! I was euphoric.

I could hardly sleep that night and was out, walking the streets of Paris at dawn. Marvellous. The time dragged by slowly but it came to pass, and there was Doris, dressed in a floral frock, standing beside the river like a dream vision that had acquired superb substance. I'd had time to think what we might do and asked her to come to the Bois de Bologne where we could get a boat and row the day away. She agreed. She was all affirmation. I had never met anybody like that before. She was so positive. We strolled to the Bois and I hired a boat and we rowed through the luscious greenery of the tree-draped lake. I rowed, she watched and talked. I stopped the boat and we sat together, our hands sometimes teasing the smooth surface of the water. We embraced, nothing explosive, but a long embrace. I explored her body with my hands — damp from the water. I felt her lovely breasts and her slim waist and her hips. It was idyllic. I was very definitely in love with her.

In the evening we went back to my hotel. Being flush, financially and emotionally, I ordered a bottle of champagne for the room and we drank it together. I had never had champagne before but it didn't go to my head and I was conscious of a startling clarity as we sat in the room, sometimes looking through the white shutters at the street below. Bliss. Everything seemed in slow motion, like a special effect in the movies, and she glided to the bed and lay back on it. I knew what to do and went over to her and caressed her. She pulled the curtains, undressed, and got under the covers. I followed suit and entered her warm, welcoming body. I don't know if I put up a great performance as I didn't ask her, but I do know that at that moment it was the most fulfilling thing that had ever happened to me. She was grand; her body was its own reward. After the sudden orgasmic rush I held on to her, wishing I could tell her what she meant to me. I think she knew, though. I think she knew.

On the third post-Doris day she had to get the train from Paris *en route* to London. Then she would fly to America. I went to the station with her to see her off. I was crazy about her. I was wretched at the thought of never seeing her again. We stood beside the train and she kissed me in a friendly rather than passionate way.

'How old are you?' she asked.

I blushed.

'How old are you?' I countered.

'Twentynine.'

Thirteen years older than me.   No wonder she was a bit more aware of the world and its promise than I was.

'I'm twentyfive,' I lied.

She smiled in that unforgettably charming way of hers.   Then she got onto the train and I waited until it moved and I waved to her and I walked back to my hotel cursing the loss of her.   For it was a permanent loss, I knew that.   I never saw her again and I knew then that I would never see her again.   The light had gone out of Paris for me and the days that followed were ghastly.   Paris had become a dull old place like Edinburgh.   Just streets and people. Even the paintings failed to move me.   I was in an advanced state of melancholia.   I moped around in my hotel and, with nothing better to do, composed my first-ever poem.   It was a rather clumsy sonnet and I didn't even utilise the Doris/Paris rhyme.   I had forgotten all about it (though not about her) when I came across my first poem in some old papers.   This is it:

> *No city could no justice to our love*
> *For love is international, not bound*
> *By language; yet it helped that it was found*
> *In Paris for here underneath the mauve*
> *Sky one is open to the hidden truth,*
> *To the atmosphere, even to the sound*
> *Of other voices so easily found*
> *In the streets and the perpetual tower above.*
> *Yet you, Doris, you surpassed even this.*
> *Your presence was a glimpse of ecstasy.*
> *You gave your gift of warm seductive joy*

And I took all your presents with a kiss.
I was astonished when you came to me:
You were a woman with an awkward boy.

As a poem it makes me cringe a bit now, but, for the record, there it is as it was.   The first poem and memorable to me because of the experience it attempted to express.   I cherish it as a reminder of that.

When I was going home to Edinburgh, I met a French girl on the London to Edinburgh train.   Not a patch on Doris.   She asked me, after some preliminary patter, '*Qui est votre vedette favourite—*'   I said 'Come again?', then I twigged that 'star' must have a cinematic connotation in French too (at least I learned *something* about the language).   I smiled and told her my favourite star was Brigitte Bardot.   She said my French was quite good.   If I'd told her the truth and said my only star then was Doris, she wouldn't have known what I was talking about.   That, though, is the way with secrets.

THE CANDLE MAKER'S DREAM

THE CANDLEMAKER'S DREAM

John Gordon was not exactly the village idiot — witness his sheer dedication to the craft of candlemaking — but the villagers felt his general behaviour to be idiotic in the extreme. He never seemed to know what any given object was intended for and if there was a wrong way of using something then that would be John Gordon's way. As he was a compulsive collector, he had ample opportunity to demonstrate his bizarre habits. From his father, who had been a candlemaker before him, John had inherited a large house with a large garden and an enormous shed, and it was in this shed he plied his trade. He lived by candlelight — both personally and professionally — and his only concession to these modern times was a colourful innovation in the design of candles. For John Gordon's candles were no ordinary common-or-garden candles but massive multicoloured columns of wax. As the villagers disdained such an ancient source of light, the tourists who came to the picturesque village were his only customers and they did not use the candles except for decoration.

It was quite normal (or had come to be accepted as such) to see John in his garden, when he came out of his shed, with a golf club in his hands. Only he didn't use it to improve his swing: he didn't play golf. Instead, he insisted that a golf club, rather than a scythe, was the best way of keeping long grass in its place. He also had a set of bowls though he didn't bowl. He threw them the length of his garden (quite a length) claiming that this was his method of keeping fit. What with his regular golf-clubbing of the grass and his bowl-throwing he had attained a remarkable degree of fitness, for, though he looked a man of fifty, John Gordon was known to be nearer three score years and ten.

Appropriately, too, for John was bible mad. He didn't attend church but was crazy about the bible —or just plain crazy, most of the the villagers would have said. When out walking he always carried his dear father's old bible and would continually read from it. He didn't listen to the radio or watch the television because he had neither. He had his good book and was contemptuous of the villagers for their creature comforts — their deep freezers and electric fires. John's aim in life, as far as the locals could discern an aim, was to be completely self-sufficient.

No one had ever been inside his big house. There was no need for any man to come to read his meter, for John lit his house entirely by the light of his beloved candles. There was no need for anyone to deliver groceries to his home because John lived on water and the vegetables he grew in his garden. He did make money from his candles but what he did make was used to buy materials for making yet more candles. Locals who suggested he was overproductive were always given the same answer: 'You'll see. One day you'll see.' This enigmatic response was treated as one more proof of John's idiocy.

Apart from his prolific candlemaking, John's other great activity was cutting wood for his fire. He was forever foraging in the local woods for logs then bringing them back to his garden to saw them into smaller logs. It was observed by the villagers that no human being could ever live long enough to burn all the logs that John Gordon had cut, but, again, they put it all down to the candlemaker's eccentricity. It was part of his nature, they reasoned, to store things up. Yet, though the villagers laughed at John and sometimes shouted supp-osedly witty remarks at him, they accepted him as part of the village.　He was, in his own strange way, a local institution.　When tourists came they would be told of the uniquely beautiful candles produced in John Gordon's garden shed.

Because the village was so lovely more and more people wanted to come to spend their summers in it.　There were rivers and lakes for fishing and the local mountainous hills provided spectacular scenery. When the tourist influx became so great that it exhausted the local supply of bed-and-breakfast establishments, the local authorities decided to build a caravan site in the village.　This way they could accommodate many visitors and receive a good rent from them.　The local shopkeepers and publicans were delighted at the idea for they saw their summers being more lucrative than ever.　John Gordon, however, was aghast.　The caravan site was to be set in a sprawling field adjacent to John Gordon's big house.

The village butcher told John his fears were groundless.　'You'll sell even more candles and you'll become a rich man.'

'I don't want to be rich,' the old man replied.　'There is no place for rich men in the kingdom of heaven.'

'There is a place for rich men in the village,' the butcher opined.

'To hell with the village,' John told him.

'Oh, to hell with you, you old fool,' was the butcher's parting shot.

He didn't much care for John anyway, on account of his persistent refusal to buy butcher meat.　He had once explained to John that men cannot live on vegetables alone and had been treated to a choice mouthful of unbiblical language.

What irked John Gordon about the proximity of the caravan site was the noise that emanated from　the place.　Visitors seemed to come to their all-mod.-cons. caravans so they could listen to their confounded radios and watch their infernal television sets.　Worst of all were the children.　They were constantly coming up to his shed and shouting rude remarks, then asking for free candles.　'What d'you want so many candles for, mister,' they would scream.　At first

John told them 'You'll see.   Someday you'll see.'   But he came to realise they were not worth talking to.   They were rough uncouth foul-mouthed boys from the city, not worth a candle.   As far as he was concerned they should go back home.   One lad, though, was different, or at least John took him to be different.   He was a twelve-year-old boy called Sandy with red hair and a face full of freckles. He was quiet and didn't come to taunt or throw insults that hurt as much as thrown stones.   He came to watch John work at his candles and praised the old man's craft and said he thought it was 'magic'.   He said he thought the colours John blended into his big wax pillars were magnificent and he came again and again.   John got to the stage where he felt impatient if a day passed without young Sandy sticking his red hair though the door to ask if he could watch.

One day he asked John an unexpected question.   'Is it true you can throw a bowl the length of the garden?' His eyes were wide and innocent and John felt touched.

'Sure,' he said with considerable pride and he came outside his shed and picked up a bowl and, like an expert athlete, punted it from one end of the garden to the other.

'That's magic,' Sandy assured him. 'And is it true you can cut your grass with a golf club?'

No sooner had he said this than John began to show him how he swung the club so it cropped the tops off the grass.

'And is it true you have lots and lots of candles to light up your house and lots and lots of logs to heat your house — like in the olden days?'

John hesitated, for he was reluctant to let anyone see the inside of his house.   But the boy looked so sweet and genuinely interested that he relented.   He took Sandy into the big house and showed him how everywhere there were candles and piles of expertly cut logs.

The boy seemed to suppress a smile, but affirmed that it was all magic.   'Yes, it is a bit of magic,' John agreed.   'And one day they'll

65

all know it is magic.' And the boy could not help but notice that, though it was light still, some candles were lit and that the candlelight shone on what he knew were religious pictures.

When they came out John Gordon felt a younger man. He was exhilarated, sure there was hope in the world. He patted Sandy on the head and asked him to come again. Then, as he was going towards the shed, he saw there were people in it. Young people. They were rushing out of the shed now with armfuls of John Gordon's candles. In a flash John knew what had happened. Sandy, his young friend, had got him into the house so his friends could gain entrance to the open sacred shed and take as many of the precious candles as they could lay hands on.

'You young swine!' John shouted at Sandy who was already running towards the caravan site. 'You little monster!'

But Sandy, who thought he was well out of harm's way, was not without the gift of verbal retaliation. 'You, you're a stupid old man. Fancy using candles to light your house. You're mad. You're round the bend. You're crackers.'

As Sandy's tirade continued, John Gordon, enraged at the injustice of it all, bent down and picked up a log he had sawn that morning. He held it firmly in his right hand and flung it with all his might in the direction of his young tormentor. There was a terrible howl of pain as the log, after spinning through the air, came to a fearful stop against the freckled forehead of the boy. Uproar spread like wildfire, and the caravan site became alive with indignation. One smallish man, with red hair like Sandy's, looked at the damage done to his son, ascertained the source of the — to him — unprovoked attack and advanced menacingly towards John Gordon.

The old candlemaker guessed that an assault was about to be made against his person and he tensed himself. He was still strong and Sandy's father was much smaller, if also much younger, than him. Furthermore, John Gordon was in a mood to do battle against the forces of evil. He took up his golf club as his staff and prepared himself. The smaller man hesitated only for a second then sprang forward. Perhaps Sandy's father meant only to subdue the candlemaker before taking him to the police, but when he received an excruciating blow to the waist from the golf club he had no alternative but to fight.

Realising that this would be no easy encounter, he steeled himself with the thought of his son's injury. His opponent had used foul means rather than fair so he would do the same. He thrust close into John Gordon's body and rammed his forehead into John Gordon's face. The old man reeled back, stunned by the force of the blow, and before he could recover he was viciously punched to the ground. Once down he felt sharp stabbing pains as feet began to cut into his face and, finally, when he was conscious of nothing but agony, he lost consciousness.

John Gordon never recovered from that attack. In many ways, the locals felt, it was just as well, for his position in the village would have been untenable. He had gone too far. The police investigated the incident and as John Gordon clung onto a twilight kind of life for three weeks it was agreed that no charge of manslaughter would be brought against a rightly outraged father defending his son against a crazy old man. Yes, they knew all about John Gordon and his strange ways, and, with hindsight, thought it inevitable that he would come to such an end.

What they didn't know about was the dream of John Gordon. Among his personal papers was a document, a testament written in a scrawl, which read:

> *'One day the waters on the earth here will dry up in a great drought and their devilish lights will stop flowing and fail in their homes and darkness will be cast upon the face of the deep and the people will cry out for the Spirit of God to move upon the face of the waters. And they will come to John Gordon for they will fear the dark and John Gordon will say "Let there be Light," and there will be light from his myriad multicoloured*

candles.   And they will want heat, and they will have no heat, and John Gordon will say "Let there be heat" and there will be heat from John Gordon's myriad logs.   And there will be a great gathering of love for John Gordon, for the Lord hath deemed it so.   And the much loved John Gordon will be praised for his great wisdom and he will be a prophet honoured in his own land.'

As the locals looked at this, at the old candlemaker's handwriting, and saw the massive piles of candles and logs he had saved for them over the years, they saw that the dream of John Gordon had perhaps come as a relief for the nightmare they had imposed upon him.

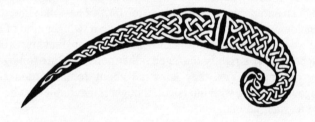

SEE YOU

Albert was taking his customary constitutional up Constitution Road when he decided to pop in for a pint. Just like that. He fancied himself as the impulsive type and felt that popping in for a pint unannounced was the sort of thing an impulsive type might get up to. Unpremeditated actions like that came secondnaturally to him. He was not a worrier. He had, in fact, nothing to worry about. No money. No bank account. No mortgage. No motor-car. No creditcard. No nothing. Nevertheless he liked to feel he was a free agent. Able to go where he liked.

So he pushed open the oak door and swaggered in. He was a big chap. Big enough to swagger into pubs and confident enough to observe the impact of his entrance. People turned to look at him. At least he expected them to. People made way at the bar. He expected that too. He was accustomed to attention. Had come to expect it. So there he was, stood at the bar, eyes raised in expectation of instant attention. He drummed his fingers on the polished surface of the oak bar. It had been recently wiped and was still slightly wet.

—— Pint please.

He liked the alliteration.

—— Pint please pal.

He was pleased with the plosives.

—— Pint please pal I'm parched.

The barman looked up at him as well he might as Albert was some eight inches taller than him.

—— Pint?

—— Please pal.

—— Coming up.

Albert felt good. Warm and cosy. He looked into the mirror behind the bar and smirked. Smugly. He smiled to himself. He felt on top of the world. The pint was presented, paid for, and despatched. Promptly despatched.

—— Same again son.

—— Already?

Albert narrowed his eyes.

—— Why not?

Albert could, when he wanted to, inject a note of menace into his voice. It went with his size. The barman grasped the significance of this vocal phenomenon instantly.

—— I was only asking sir. No offence.

Albert's face relaxed into a smile.

—— None taken.

He pursed his lips. He rolled his finger on the wooden surface of the bar. He drummed his fingers. He wished he had someone to talk to. And lo, as if in answer to his wish he heard a voice, an enigmatic voice, a voice sweeping into his consciousness as if from afar.

—— Albert you bugger!

His neck jerked back. He turned to confront the rude intruder. And he saw. And he liked what he saw. It was Sammy, a friend from way back. A chap he had worked with once many moons ago when the two of them had been employed on the same building site in casual labour and had shared digs together. He stuck out his hand. It was a large hand and completely contained the other hand.

—— How's it going Sammy?   Good to see you pal.

—— How's it going with you?

—— Doing away.   Doing away.

—— Are you working yet Albert?   Or are you still idle?

Albert raised his eyebrows.   Of course he wasn't working but he wan't going to tell Sammy this because he did not know what position Sammy himself was in.   He was going to play it by ear.

—— Great news that.   What are you doing Albert?

Albert thought for a while and while his cerebral cogs were whirling round he stalled for time by asking whether Sammy wanted a pint and, after observing an affirmative expression, pointing at the barman then purchasing the pint then passing the present to his old pal.

—— I'm a chauffeur now, Sammy.   This is my day off.   I'm chauffeur to the Duke of Berlochead in fact.   Not a bad number, I'll tell you that son.   Plenty of money to put in the tail.   And time off.   I'm just dressed casual like just now because these are just clothes to nick about in.

Sammy looked at him and nodded vigorously.

—— Same with me Albert.   I'm just dressed casual today.

—— What are you doing then Sammy?

Sammy put down his pint and inhaled some pubfuggy air.   Then he looked straight at Albert.

—— I'm doing fine matter of fact Albert.   I've got my own business.   Contracting, buying and selling, that sort of thing.   Got a partnership with two other blokes.   Well, they put up the capital and I supplied the old know-how.   Know what I mean?

Albert remembered how much difficulty Sammy had had even digging a hole.   But he took his turn to nod in agreement.

—— Sure.

—— I've got my own car and a new house Albert.   Nice they are.

Albert looked into Sammy's eyes insistently.

—— Listen, Sammy, could you drive me somewhere today then? It's an appointment.

Sammy picked up his pint and gulped down some of the flattish contents. Which movement gave Albert the opportunity to ogle the shabby nature of Sammy's knitwear. He looked hard up.

—— I'm sorry Albert. Any other time old son. I would if I could. I had a brush with the law last week. Out at a champagne party, you know. There was this dolly and me. Great it was. But after a couple of bottles of the old champers and what-have-you I was a bit pissed and the law nabbed me. Asked me to breathe into the balloon and that was that. Sine die. Can't use the car.

—— Pity about that.

—— Still, I can't complain Albert. I've got this boat, you know. It's down on the coast at the moment, at Captain's Bay. I'm going to sail to Ibiza in it.

Albert allowed himself a sceptical look.

—— On your own?

—— Of course. Well I met this geezer at the private golf club I go to — the old handicap's down to eleven — and he sold me the boat. I won't say how much but you can take it it set me back a few bob. He's been to Ibiza in it himself. So it should be fine.

—— I've been down to Captain's Bay and seen the boats. Never seen you there Sammy. And a mate of mine, Dougie Gregor, goes down there regular.

—— Dougie? Know him well.

—— He's never said he's seen you there.

Sammy finished his beer and banged the glass sharply on the polished barsurface.

—— Well, Dougie probably goes down to make a few bob. Probably helps out. I go there in my spare time. To get away from it all. When I've got any. Spare time that is.

—— Drink Sammy?

Albert was aware that it was Sammy's round.

—— Could you get it Albert?   I didn't bring any cash with me.   I use the old chequebook you know.

—— The bar will cash a cheque.

—— Not worth it really.   It doesn't matter.   Not worth it for such a small amount.   You get them Albert and I'll repay the compliment some other time.

Albert had enough money for two more drinks and had been hoping to scoff them himself.   Still, he paid up.

—— So you're a chauffeur Albert?   Didn't know you could drive?

Albert couldn't.

—— Advanced driver now Sammy.   You want to see this Rolls I run about in.   Beauty.   Like driving on air.   And you want to see the Duke's wife.   Patricia's her name.   About half his age but then he's loaded.   A real beauty I'm not kidding.   I've been knocking her off.

—— Really?

—— Know what she says to me after I'd been there a week?

Sammy shook his head.   And started on the new pint.

—— She says: fancy a ride?   That's what she said.

Sammy shook his wise head more slowly this time as if to indicate that he was only too well aware that such things happen in this world of saints and sinners.

—— I'm telling you.   She says: fancy a ride?   I says: yes.   She says: see you upstairs in half an hour.   So I goes upstairs in half an hour.   And right enough she's lying in bed just waiting for it.   You know.   And the Duke's away for the weekend on some grouse shoot or something like that.   Golf or guns or something like that.   And there's me banging his wife.   Fantastic eh?

Sammy nodded.   Then suddenly he shot his sleeve up as if to look at his watch.   There was no watch there but he looked seriously at Albert.

—— Been great to see you Albert but I must dash.   I've got a plane to catch at the airport on the hour.   I'll have to get a taxi.   Just came in here to wet my whistle.

—— Fine then Sammy.   See you again.

—— See you.

And Albert watched Sammy dash out of the door.   And he finished his drink and looked at the clock.   It was nearly signing-on time.   So he said goodbye to the barman and walked back into Constitution Road and made his way down towards the docks where someone had told him they might be taking on men today.

THE COCK AND BULL STORY

It was going to be a whole new way of life. A clean sweep. Dave was quite clear about that. A new beginning. A fond farewell to the old. A new set of values. A new challenge. A house not architecturally new but different enough to be novel. Dave had it all cleared up in his mind. The skies would look new. The air would feel new. New rain would fall on new ground. There would be newness everywhere. He and Linda would be renewed as a couple, re-made in the image Dave had gripped in the vice inside his head. All their lives, almost, Dave and Linda had been city-dwellers. All their married life they had agreed on how restricting, how destructive, how dustily claustrophobic city life was. They had hated it, but done nothing. Despised it, but tolerated it.

Now everything was different. Ater three years of trying they had a baby. Having seen many marriages crumbling on the bricks that grasped people in cities, having watched love affairs break up on unswept pavements — they were not going to let it happen to them. Not now they had a child to care for. Dave was sure that the child had come as a saviour to rescue their marriage. And he was going to move, going to put miles of countryside between him and the city.

He had been lucky to find the place they were going to move into. It was a massive old farmhouse rented from an ancient amiable farmer whose memories spanned two world wars. The farmer was not interested in agriculture: he simply owned the land he walked on and gazed into the skies above remembering dogfights, or inventing them. He was happy to rent the big farmhouse to a young couple, with a baby too, because he insisted that he was happiest when someone was there to enjoy the space and the view. No, it hadn't been inhabited for some time. But the people from the little town nearby were too lazy to stray far from their own backyards. That's what the farmer said. Technically they could be put out at six months notice, but the farmer winked at Dave and said that as long as he was alive Dave and Linda could rest assured they were secure. As old soldiers proverbially never die, Dave thought it worth the risk. He would leave his city flat for this big grand dream of a farmhouse. Not only four times the size of his city flat but half the rent. It was irresistible.

Dave was to get the place ready and he was jubilant at his good fortune. Not just the ridiculously low rent of the place but the place itself. There was a green field at the back of the house that led to a wood that in turn dipped sharply downhill until it was intercepted by a little stream concealed by an impenetrable tangle of branches. They were black, robbed by the winter of the warmth of their leaves. From the stream there was a magnificent view of a landscape of ploughed fields which absorbed the sun. It was idyllic, Dave thought to himself. Of course he knew that farmworkers worked the fields and looked after the cows during the day. But to people accustomed to the din and whine and clatter of a city the splutter of a tractor or the groans of animals combined to a freshness and sweetness that Dave was determined to live with.

Three miles from the farmhouse there was a little town where they could get special things. Food was brought by a delivery van so there was no problem there. Still, Dave told Linda, they could go to the little town for an evening if they fancied a drink or a meal out. Of course, Dave added, such visits would be few and far between because they were leaving the city to extend their personalities not to become provincials. Yet once in a while he supposed they would nip into the little town and relax over a beer and chat to the locals. But they would not become involved with the locals. They both agreed on that. Linda said that living in the city had kept them apart from each other. Dave was always going out for a drink on the grounds that he could not be restricted to a flat. Now there would be no excuses. They would have each other.

Their child was born in January and they called her Janet. Linda thought that 'January' would make a lovely unusual name but Dave gently disagreed. With a bit of pre-prepared erudition he told her that January was traditionally the month of the Italian god Janus. Janus: the god of doors, the god of two faces. No, it was not a good idea to saddle children with conspicuously eccentric names. They had to live with them for the rest of their lives. Linda listened to Dave's reasons and agreed. This was an omen for Dave. Usually disagreements ended up in shouting, screaming matches. When this one didn't, when Linda softly succumbed to his argument, he was surer than ever that the child was the saviour of their marriage. Their life was about to fructify.

When Janet was two months old Linda felt ready to move into the farmhouse. Dave had already moved most of their stuff down and had been commuting from the farmhouse to the flat getting everything ready for the final move. And when he came back to the city he stayed in with her now. Every night. Showed no inclination to go out for a drink. He talked on and on about the farmhouse and Linda was glad. A child and loving husband. The warm milk dribbled from her breast and she sighed in utter satisfaction.

In one special sense Dave was lucky and he knew it. He did not have to be tied down in any one place on account of his work. He was a potter and quite moderately successful at that. Friends assured him he was going places. Admittedly his work was un-ashamedly commercial but if aesthetic friends chided him for his lack of integrity he would reply that he had no intention of crucifying his wife and child on the strength of his temperament. So he was glad to be away from such friends. He would concentrate on building up business for his pottery. Already he had set himself up at the farmhouse. He had one massive room on the ground floor for a workshop. It was what he had always wanted. Room to stand back and stare at his finished pots.   Space in which to create his pots.   He could prepare displays for shops, photograph them, and drum up business.   He could arrange groups for exhibitions.   It was almost too good to be true, Dave thought.   He lit a fag and puffed out clouds of satisfaction.

March was the month of the final move.   It was also the beginning of spring round the farmhouse.   Dave could see that plants were beginning to emerge from the ground although as yet he knew next to nothing about growing things.   Still he could respond.   He liked to go down to the stream and walk carefully among the fragile snowdrops, listening to the birds and the water, thinking of renewal. The only thing that disturbed his peace was the thought that it had taken him so long to get the hell out of the city.   He was now thirty.   Which made him five when he moved to the city from a seaport.   And he had been twentyfive years in the city and hated it all.   But there was no point in crying over spilt milk.   Instead he suddenly dashed up the little slope, pelted across his own green field, ran over to the cows in the barn opposite the farmhouse.   They gazed back at him, rolling their langorous heads, chomping their turnips, spluttering through their noses, and dribbling with their tongues.   Dave liked them.   They were inoffensive.   Unlike people.   He knew he was going to be happy.

On the day that Linda moved in with baby Janet, Dave bought a pair of hens.   He had thought of starting off his country life with something bigger but then decided to start from the bottom.   Hens were small and attractive and they laid eggs.   That was something a townee could understand.   And the two hens that Dave bought proved tremendously efficient at laying eggs.   They produced one every day.   And always in the same spot.   Not in the hen house. They seemed to scorn that.   But just outside the door.   It was as if there was a deal on.   Every morning Dave would go to his back door and throw out henfood to the hens.   And every morning they would oblige him with one egg each.   Laid near his back door.   Always in the same spot. Beautiful eggs. Brown and firm outside, succulent when cooked. Which made Dave ambitious to graduate onto proper farming. There would be a time, he thought, when he might well handle pigs and maybe even cows and bulls. It might happen. He would certainly get to grips with the soil. He had the hands for clay: perhaps he had green fingers too.

Linda thought the new home was wonderful. It was not, of course, new in the strict sense. In fact it must have had quite a history over a couple of hundred years. But they knew nothing of the past of the farmhouse, only what it meant to them now. The farmer, when they saw him, said nothing about who had lived there. So Dave and Linda would imagine what it must have been like before electricity and motorcars brought people from the city. They would make up a wood fire and watch the sparks and spluttering flicks of flame and see in the flames a golden past and a golden future in which they were prominent. Dave would see more children and wealth. Linda would see a hazy undefined kind of happiness.

As Dave made his own hours of work they had no fixed timetable. Except that each evening they would have an elaborate meal. A complicated dish with a good wine. Dave did once remark on the incongruity of moving to the country for the simple life and then pampering themselves with gastronomic excess. But so what: they would make their own rules. They were happy.. Dave believed they had, in each other, everything there was worth having. They went to bed.

In April Dave had to go away for a week to attend a conference of arts and crafts. He found these long-winded, self-congratulatory, pompous, unending, incestuous gatherings tiresome. But he had his career to think about and anything he did to promote his name helped. He needed money, pottery was his sole means of income: simple as that. If he could improve his earning power by spending a week or whatever discussing the validity of the crafts in a materialistic world, fair enough. It was a small price to pay for a chance of success. Naturally he felt a bit worried about leaving Linda with a four-month-old baby on her own in a big isolated farmhouse, but he put the disquiet down to being conditioned in a city. She would be perfectly all right. He had stocked up the fridge with food that would last for weeks and had bought boxes of tinned food so she could not possibly lack anything. True, she would be car-less, as he intended to drive to the conference. But then he asked one of the few friends he had made in the little town, a friendly bloke called Brian, to drop in just to make sure she was fine. The man agreed at once with a friendliness which made Dave think how much more co-operative country folk were than town people. In the country, people were used to driving several miles to get from one point to the other, so that a drive of six miles (from the little town to the farmhouse and back) to help out, seemed no bother at all. Dave felt that after all he might enjoy his week away. These conferences were pretty alcoholic affairs and he was partial to the odd boozeup. So he left his wife and child and his green field and his stream and his farmhouse and drove away with a crystal clear conscience.

It was a different story coming back. His head seemed ready to split like a stood-on orange. There had been infinitely more consumption of spirits than exposition of views and the sessions of drinking had been intensive. He had spent far too much and in the last couple of days had remembered his old nausea with cities. The perpetual petrol stench. The racket that went on nonstop. The shouting and rushing and screaming and pushing. He was more than glad to be driving home to his farmhouse and his wife and his child and his green field and his stream. Though his head was beating he knew a meal and a bottle of wine — a hair of the dog — would renew him. And, after all, there was one consolation. He had met several gallery and shop people at the conference. He had firm offers for exhibitions and orders. It was successful in that sense. He was told he was going places (he had always been told that). But the people bored him. He was still infatuated with the open-ness of the country people. Conference chatter about cars and holidays in California and weekends in the country made him yawn.

At five he was back at the farmhouse. Janet was still awake, Linda was making a meal. She came across and kissed him when he came in. He went across to the baby and kissed her. Linda surveyed him with a smile.

—— Enjoy yourself?

—— You must be joking. Talk and drink and then more drink. But I do have some definite orders and some shows arranged.

—— That's marvellous then. I'm glad you decided to go.

—— I hope that doesn't mean you didn't miss me.

She renewed her smile.

—— Of course I did. So did Janet. But you must be hungry.

—— Nothing elaborate.

—— I've made a salad and an Italian meal to follow.

—— Well, I'll have the salad and Italian wine without the food. My stomach couldn't stand it.

—— Right.

She went into the kitchen. Dave thought he'd go out and chop some wood. He could see that while he had been away Linda had been using coal for the fire. He preferred wood and thought that chopping some would do him good. He went out and onto the green field at the back when suddenly, astonishingly, one of the hens rushed at him and attacked him viciously. He was astounded. Surely after a week hens did not regress and become predatory creatures with a penchant for human flesh. But as he used his foot to shove the hen away he noticed immediately. Even he, townee, could tell that the creature now waddling away in retreat was not a hen but a cockerel. What the hell had happened? He ran back to the farmhouse.

—— Linda!

—— Just about ready love.

Dave stormed into the kitchen.

—— What's that bloody cockerel doing out there?

She looked surprised then her smile came back.

—— Brian.

—— Brian?

—— Yes: Brian gave us it.

—— What Brian?

—— The Brian you asked to drop in.

—— The Brian who mends fences? Him! You mean that Brian?

—— Who else?

—— What the hell do we want a cockerel for? The animal's a bloody lunatic anyway. It attacked me.

—— I'm sorry about that, but Brian said it was fine getting unfertilised eggs from our hens but that we'd be better producing chickens.

—— Why?

—— So we could eat them, of course.

—— I'm not going to cultivate live creatures then eat them!

—— Don't be ridiculous, Dave. That's how country people get their food. It's a bit daft to live in the country then send off for a frozen chicken when you can have your own chicken fresh.

—— But it's only April. Christmas isn't for months.

—— You don't have to eat them only at Christmas and anyway chickens have to........develop.

—— Well, I'm going to give bloody Brian his bloody cockerel back.

—— You can't, David. He'd be hurt. He was very thoughtful. He helped. He even mended the fence round the back. Without taking payment. He was very nice.

Dave looked at her then realised that he was making too much fuss over a trivial incident. He wasn't hurt after all. And Brian was obviously demonstrating a genuine friendliness. Dave was acting like a townee.

—— Look, Linda, I'm sorry about all this fuss. It's the......

—— I know: the conference and the drink and the late nights. That's the city for you.

He nodded, lit a fag, and blew out a vigorous sigh. Then he sat down on the couch in front of the fire. He would get the wood later. Just now he was tired. It was the conference, the drink and the late nights. Within five minutes he fell asleep. He dreamed about cock fights and heard the biblical cock crowing his name and then he woke to the sound of a cockerel screaming. Only it wasn't. It was Janet. She was howling because she was wet and Linda was changing her with some exasperation. Dave was too tired to comment. He supposed everyone would get a bit ratty after changing babies day and night. He thought his best plan for the evening was to say little and simply respond to being back at the farmhouse. That night, when he went to bed he felt Linda coldly respond to his touch then move away from him. He slept badly, too, convinced he could hear the arrogant cackle of the cockerel.

When Dave recovered from the return from the conference he was his old self again. His body returned to the peace of the country. He thanked Brian for the gift of the cockerel and in exchange presented him with a beautiful pot. Brian was grateful. Yes, Dave told Brian, he could see that breeding chickens would be a good idea. Further, Dave told Brian to drop in anytime — which he did. Soon they became friendly. Brian was a dark, weatherbeaten man with strong hands from putting up fences. At times he was effortlessly rural. But, as Dave found out through conversation, Brian was not a hundredpercent countryman. No. He had once been a student and had been thrown out of not one but two universities. Which left him convinced that he had been persecuted by a bunch of middleclass hidebound academics. After the two dismissals he had decided to give up the pursuit of learning so he could earn his living by the strength in his hands.

Though normally open and friendly, Brian could sometimes brood for long periods. He now never read books, never entertained serious searching conversation. Instead he would retreat into a blatant self-pity, complaining that his intellect had atrophied with his years in the country. Whenever Dave tried to make a serious point Brian would turn down the sides of his mouth and glance sideways, a signal that Dave read as tacit condemnation. Brian would let him know that he understood the discussion, disapproved, but would not participate. Still, for all these faults Dave liked Brian, who was about ten years older than himself with a real capacity to exude earthiness. He was, after all, a person who had made a countryman out of himself.

Summer was golden in the farmhouse. Flowers were everywhere. Yellow, red, purple, blue — the colours ballooned about the grass. And the sun reared its beautiful big head for almost the whole day and still burned fiercely up to the minute when night came. Dave and Linda would stand out in the green field and watch the sun, a huge sphere of flaming gas, flatten out on top of the horizon — their horizon — before it put the world around them to bed. They would bathe in the warmth that seeped all around them then go back to the farmhouse and light a wood-fire. The baby was more content now, too, as if acknowledging her first summer. They would bring her out to the green field during the day so she could get the warmth. Dave told Linda that this child would surely be happy, for her first memories would be of natural growing things. And the sounds were the sounds of cows and birds: natural sounds. Even the harsh wailing of the cockerel seemed to fit into the scheme of things.

The cockerel was quite well disposed to Dave by now. It came in the morning for its food, though never so confidently as the strutting hens. Clearly, Dave thought, the cockerel was more intelligent than the hens. And while the hens still didn't like their henhouse, preferring the freedom of the green field, the cockerel would hide itself in the little wooden hut frequently.

Because it was summer and eveything was going so well Dave thought he would hold his first party at the farmhouse. He would invite friends from the city and perhaps some people from the little town. Brian could see to that, for he was in constant contact with the people who lived in the little town. Apart from Brian, Dave did not know many of the locals though he had passed a few half hours with them over a pint of beer now and then. For the party he would buy several dozen cans of beer and a dozen bottles of sparkling white wine. If his guests wanted more then they could bring along their own special favourite.

If one thing worried Dave it was Linda's coldness to him. He was too inhibited to discuss it with her. At first he was seriously concerned, then he realised it must be the effect of the birth of Janet. A delayed reaction of course, for Linda had been incredibly loving when they first came to the farmhouse. But he could wait. There was no need to be impatient in the country. The seasons came round and there was constant birth and rebirth. Dave reminded himself that he was part of this seasonal life. He would wait for the renewal of passion in Linda. There was no point in worrying her.

On the morning of the party Dave took baby Janet into the little town. There was little point in having her in the house and Brian had found them an absolutely reliable babysitter. Brian and Dave had a good pub lunch of fresh beef sandwiches and beer so their stomachs would be primed for the coming party. Brian would, of course, stay the night at the farmhouse as would the guests who came from the city. The locals could easily get back to the little town, though if they were incapable of driving Dave was sure he could find room for everyone.

The party was scheduled to begin at five. It was a gorgeous evening, bright yellow with a deep orange horizon and the green field bristling in the intensity of sunlight. Dave had mowed the green field a few weeks before and it was in excellent trim for sitting on. In the middle of the green field was a big tree stump that could be used as a table. On this Dave placed half a dozen bottles of wine. Which left another six cooling in the kitchen plus the beer and whatever the guests brought. However, only half a dozen people turned up, all of them from the city. With Brian and Linda and Dave himself that meant nine people. Those guests who couldn't make it from the city phoned to say their car had broken down or a relative had turned up unexpectedly or some business had cropped up. Dave hid his disappointment well and made everybody welcome. The six that turned up — three couples — brought additional drink so there was no shortage of liquid cheer. They could all get down to the serious business of enjoying themselves.

And enjoy themselves they did. Dave got his record player through to the kitchen so the music could be heard on the green field. Brian proved to be the life and soul of the party. To Dave's surprise Brian turned out to be a dab hand at occult tricks and tales. He produced a set of Tarot cards and told all present their fortunes. He could also read palms. And he did this with such panache and such conviction that he became the exclusive centre of attraction. His predictions were all optimistic so no one had cause to curse. Dave was told he would find wealth. Linda that she was on the brink of ecstatic happiness. When Linda blushed Dave laughed openly. He was amused that she should seem to take such nonsense seriously.

By the time the occult games were exhausted it was midnight. Outside it was pitch black except for the band of stars covering the sky. There was still drink to be drunk. Dave was very drunk by this time but he knew he was not alone in his insobriety. Linda was flirtatious — totally out of character. She was well and truly under the influence.

With no more occult tricks to amuse the guests, Brian turned to eerie anecdotes. At first they were inoffensive and ineffective. Then he aroused the interest of everyone when he said that the farmhouse itself was a place of death. A couple of the guests giggled but Dave frowned. Linda was impressionable and Dave did not want her to hear any tales about the house that might alarm her. Dave gestured to Brian to change the subject.

—— Come on now Brian, no more fairy tales.

—— It's the truth, Dave. There was a death. One summer night. Like this. It was pretty bad, but if you don't want to hear.....

Linda pleaded with him.

—— Of course we want to hear, don't we Dave. Well I do. I'm not a little girl who's afraid of fairy stories.

Dave shrugged his shoulders. Linda was supremely confident with the drink and there was no way she could be stopped now.

—— Carry on then, Brian, but don't overdo the lurid details.

Brian gulped down a glass of whisky and smacked his lips.

—— Well, this couple lived here. A long time ago mind you. Well, one night the husband went away and when he came back he found, believe it if you like, that a bull had broken from a field and panicked and come into that field at the back somehow and found the wife and, well, gored her to death.

Dave was angry.

—— Complete rubbish. You made it up.

—— It's not a cock and bull story, Dave, but it's up to you. That's why the locals wouldn't come to your party.

Everyone giggled nervously at this remark though more from a desire to break the tension than in appreciation of Brian's story. Dave laughed too; so did Linda. So Dave decided to end the story by quickly proposing a toast to his wife and insisting that everyone recharge their glasses. And the talk turned to other things. And the talk got slower and the speech more slurred as the drink took its inexorable effect on the senses.

Dave was the first to really show the impact of the mixture of beer, white wine and whisky. One minute he felt fine, the next he rushed to the kitchen door and vomited out onto the green field. He thought he saw the cockerel move too, but no, it was only a tree rustling, a movement of green against black. When he came back, his eyes bright red and stitched with scarlet veins, he could hardly even make excuses. His head was nodding, he felt awful, but he managed to indicate that he was going upstairs to bed. Everyone else was to carry on with the party. Linda, suddenly serious, said she would come with him but he shook his head and staggered off to the staircase, the assault of which seemed Everest-like in its challenge that night.

Once his head was down on the bed Dave went into a deep pillow-spin. He felt his head whirl round and round and round until he thought he'd never sleep. But he did. For some hours. It was a fitful sleep with that cockerel disturbing his dreams and then images of a massive bull crashing into a woman. Then he woke. And realised he was still alone. He listened. No sound. Everyone must have gone to bed. But where was Linda? She must have flaked out downstairs, he thought. With a wrench he raised himself to his feet and wobbled for a couple of minutes. He was still dressed though he had no shoes on. Someone must have taken them off. He decided to see what had happened to Linda.

She wasn't in the front room, she wasn't in his workshop, she wasn't anywhere downstairs. He was puzzled: annoyed and puzzled. Then he heard a sort of cry outside. That bloody cockerel, he thought. He heard the little cry again. It pierced his drink-sodden head. On an angry impulse he decided to go out to the green field to shut the bird up. The back door was open and he walked out. Squelch: he had stepped in his stockinged feet into his own vomit of hours before. He thought he was going to be sick again. But there was the cry again. He walked towards it. And as his eyes got used to the imperceptibly lightening darkness he could make out shapes moving. Human shapes. Naked human shapes.

His first reaction was to withdraw as quickly as he could. He realised that two of the guests had opted for a bit of romantic love on the grass, which was fine by him. But he seemed rooted to the spot. He knew the face intimately. It was Linda. And hulking over her body was Brian. Linda's expression froze when she saw him.

—— Dave!

He put his hands to his head, turned, and ran into the house.

For the first week after the party Dave hardly said a word to Linda except to tell her he was considering the legal position. He felt as if someone had taken a knife and plunged it into his brain. He couldn't think of anything else but those naked shapes in the night. He was shocked. There was no word from Brian, of course, nor did Dave expect to hear from him. All Dave could hear, over and over, were those sounds that alerted him that night. He tried to black them out with drink but there was always the clarity of the morning to face and the noise of that cockerel that so resembled Linda's cries that night. Then after thirteen days of brooding he could take no more. He woke up to the sound of the cockerel and knew what to do. His blood seemed to boil within him as he dressed and he drank whisky even while he dressed.

He went downstairs and screamed at Linda.

—— You rotten cow!

—— I'm sorry. Honestly, I'm sorry.

—— You've ruined everything: the lot.

—— It just happened. I....

—— Was that the first time? Was it?

She looked alarmed.

—— There's no point in making it worse by lying. No. Once before.

In an instant he knew.

—— When I went away to that conference and that.....

He was overpowered by an image of all his plans collapsing and all because of this woman standing in front of him. This destroyer.

—— Cow!

He launched himself towards her and struck her on the side of the head. Her mouth gaped open and her hairdo fell apart. He screamed then hit her again. Tears were pouring down his face, blood down hers. And when she fell he kicked her viciously in the stomach. She was screaming too. Yelling for help. And the child in the green field heard the screams and began to cry. And the cockerel began to wail uncontrollably.

Dave rushed out into the green field and threw himself at the cockerel. He was going to strangle it. It resisted, but he twisted its neck until its head almost came off. But it wouldn't die. It seemed to throb with life. Its body twitched and it was up on its feet again. It terrified him with this seeming resurrection and he backed off. And there came another scream and Linda came out with the garden shears. He raised his hand. If she was going to kill him she would have to be fast for if he could he would strangle her as he had strangled the cockerel and there would be no resurrection out of her. Though she was not coming at him but at the cockerel. With one vicious stroke she cut its head off. Dave could only watch as the blood pumped out of the body of the cockerel, dark red spilling onto the green field. The screaming all round him had stopped but the headless body of the cockerel writhed and twisted as if it still clung to life. When it stopped Linda threw down the shears, went to the baby and picked her up.

As she passed Dave he looked away. There was blood on her face and blood on her hands and blood brushed against the baby. Her face looked hideous, as if she had been in an accident.

That Christmas Dave was on his own in the big farmhouse. On the table there was a frozen chicken still wrapped. He did not feel hungry. Instead he went into the kitchen and pottered around in the medicine cupboard. Then he came back to the table, drank some more, then staggered towards the telephone and tried desperately hard to remember the name and number of the local doctor.

A DOG'S LIFE

A DOG'S LIFE

The morphology of Dod's nose had been partly determined by the edge of a shovel. Or, as he liked to put it when asked: 'The bastards got me that time.' That was in a fight seven years before. That was before he got his driving licence back. That was when, demotorised, he had to work on a building site and watch the lorries go by. Now he was driving again, for Bubblee Brewers and happy to let the past rest, except that sometimes the nose gave him trouble with his breathing. He was aware of it, too, every time he looked in the mirror and therefore conscious of the crew who ganged up on him to do it. He had a personal mirror in the cabin of his wagon, by the side of a faded photograph of a once-famous starlet, Lustey Wenche, who, failing to explode into stardom, then collapsed into interstellar obscurity. Dod remembered her. Cathy reminded him of her.

Dod looked up into this personal mirror. Hair intact, features fine. Yes, he thought, the nose was rugged more than anything else. A badge of toughness, a medal for violent action. He was on the small side, but believed, as he constantly told people, that it's not the size of a dog in the fight but the size of the fight in a dog. He nodded at the wisdom of this. Yes, he was rugged. Still the same Dod. Still the same magician who could take care of anything in skirts. That took him back, too. Way back. At one time his life had been a succession of one-night stands with any mattress-queen who happened to be handy. Now, to be honest with himself, he was content with Cathy.

He nodded to himself in the mirror. Winked at himself. Yes, he had to admit it. The inevitable had happened or was about to happen. Dod, the old magician, was ready to settle. Dod, the teenage tearaway who had been arrested for robbery; Dod, a large part of whose army career had been spent in the glasshouse; Dod, who had several convictions for assault; Dod, a local legend for toughness; Dod had admitted it. It might be good to settle with a good woman. And Cathy was all right. Different from the others. Well-mannered. Well-spoken. He liked that. He liked women to be feminine and fragile and delicate and to leave the fags and the maniacal boozing to the men. Yes, Dod liked that. He smiled and shuffled contentedly in the driving seat.

His eyes watched the road rolling under his front wheels, but he kept to the speed limit. One loss of licence was enough. He could not take that again. And it had been unnecessary. It was not really his habit to be reckless on the road. And then in one day so much could happen. Heavy load. Tired. No overnight stop. Too many bottles of beer in the driving cabin. Too much to drink. Rush. Road recalcitrant. Sudden loss of vision. Sudden glimpse of motorcyclist on the road. Insane swerve to avoid hitting the bastard though serve him right. Crash. Bashed forehead but otherwide ok. Lifted. Charged. Drunken driving. Licence lifted. No justice. If he ever saw that motorcyclist again.....But no, it would not be worth it. It just could not happen twice. Today there was only one afternoon stop. He had a mate to pick up at Bubblee's and the two of them were to drive to a private hotel and stock it up with the old liquid assets. Piece of cake. It was early yet. Dod had set out at 5 a.m. He woke up before 5 a.m. every morning since his army days in the glasshouse. It started as an order but hardened into a habit.

The glasshouse hadn't been too bad, he told himself. Sure, it was tough. But what wasn't? He respected and revered toughness. Despised bastardry and sneakiness, yes. But real genuine honest-to-goodness toughness? You couldn't beat it. And the glasshouse got him fit.   Fighting fit.   So fighting fit in fact that each time he was let out he felt game enough to take anyone on.   And usually did.   And ended up back where he started.   Dod, the guards would say, you should live here even when your time is up.   You'll never go back to civilian life after this.   And he would laugh.   But one thing no-one could deny Dod.   No, tell a lie, two things.   His driving was excellent.   And he had considerable expertise with a rifle.   He was six-six in both eyes.   A gunman.   From way back.

He was congratulating himself on this when he swerved to let Sam heave himself up into the cabin.

—— Morning Dod.

—— Morning my old son.

—— How are you keeping?

—— Same old magician Sam.   Yourself?

—— Just doing away, Dod.   Just doing away.

Sam settled himself, Dod satisfied himself that Sam was settled and they were away.   The road was smooth and the noise of the big wagon receded and they were eventually able to talk without echoes of *What's-that* and *Can't-hear-you-speak-up.*   They talked about the things they usually talked about.   They repeated, with variations, themes they had discussed before.   They comforted each other with verbal familiarity and cared little about communicative cross-examination.   Neither was interested in contradiction.   Both cared little about candid accusations.   They were, it looked, relaxed.

Sam asked about Cathy and Dod asked about the Missus and they both enquired after each other.   Still go to the club?   Still drink as much?   Still see Wally Hamilton on Sunday night?   Still play in the darts team?   Still work for the same gaffer?   Still as randy as ever?   Still the night, the day, the morning.   Their lives were established as still.   Still the same.   All was still.   Then, business-like, Dod, captain-like turned as to a first-mate-like subordinate and asked a point of information.

—— Been to this hotel before, Sam?

—— No, by crumps, it's a new one to me.

Dod smiled to himself.   In all the time he had known Sam he had never known him to swear.   It was never *'By Christ'*, always *'By crumps'*.   Never *'bugger'* or *'bastard'*, but *'buffer'*.   He might mildly criticise some buffer or other but that was as far as his condemnation ever went.

—— New hotel then?

—— No, Dod.   It's a hotel that tried to get their beer from someone else, but had to come to us because......

—— Because this is our territory.

—— Exactly.

—— Bubblee's have worked this patch for years.

—— Long before our time Dod.

—— Don't reckon they'll be kicked out of their contract here.

—— Touch wood.

And Dod tapped Sam's head.   Sam smiled though he'd heard and felt this joke umpteen dozen hundred times.   Dod concluded the dialectic.

—— Man must look after his territory.

—— They must that Dod.

—— Man must protect what's his.

Dod changed gear as they came to a hill.   He was an excellent driver and cursed that day he had drunk too much on a job.   Dod reckoned he could outdrink most men and always had something to drink on a job, but that day he had gone too far and had crashed his lorry and lost not only his licence but his pride.   It was galling to have to be a backseat driver for a couple of years.   He wouldn't again take risks on the road.

—— Must be near here Sam.

—— Crumps, yes.

At the top of the hill they saw a sign pointing up a narrow lane. It read '*Wilf's Wonderland. The Fun Hotel*' and indicated a short drive to the promised land.

Dod noted the name. Sam read it aloud. Neither commented on it. It was a fact to digest in case they were asked to go there again. But the road *was* narrow.

—— By crumps, you'll never get a lorry up there Dod.

—— Just watch me.

This was what Dod most enjoyed about his job. A demonstration of his driving skill. Impossible angles were taken, even the most inconspicuous obstacles avoided. All with the mechanical agility of a jaguar if a jaguar could be imagined with metallic parts and oil and a willingness to wander in Wilf's Wonderland.

—— There you go.

And there they were. In the courtyard of a rather splendid little hotel. Well groomed grass. Clean walls. Sam looked impressed.

—— By crumps, but you're a clever buffer at the driving Dod.

Dod permitted a smug smile to play about his lips, as if to acknowledge the compliment. And he was savouring it and ready to open the cabin door when there was a colossally loud roar.

—— By crumps.......!

—— What the hell.....!

It was an enormous alsatian dog that suddenly appeared at their window. Leaping, barking, furiously aggressive. It made one helluva noise. And it was a brute of a dog, a huge fierce snapping creature. It twisted its ugly head as it barked and presented a pair of fangs that would make a shark envious and a tiger jealous. Dod tried to outshout it.

—— Away you big ugly beast! Get down you devil! Get out of it! Go On! Shooooh!

It is extremely doubtful if the dog heard any of this. Or the efforts of Sam.

—— Go away you buffer! Move, by crumps!

Dod eventually started the engine up, and began honking his horn, and was getting ready to reverse out of it when the owner of the hotel, an elf of a man with a voice like a foghorn, came tripping across the grass. It had to be Wilf, and his Wonderland had gotten out of hand. Yet when he got to the dog he instantly silenced it. With it under control Dod was persuaded to wind down his window to see what the man had to say. He swiftly apologised profusely.

—— I'm awfully sorry about this, lads. Bongo doesn't know how to behave with strangers yet, but he'll have to learn, won't you Bongo. This is Bongo. I'm Wilf, by the way. Welcome to Wonderland.

—— Is the dog for security?

—— Yes, actually. Well, you have to, lads, don't you. I mean, these days. You never know what's lurking round the next corner do you?

Dod looked at Wilf then at the dog.

—— You can't beat an alsatian for security, Mister Wilf. I'll tell you that.

—— You really think so? You have a pet yourself then perhaps?

—— An alsatian. Not as big as that one, right enough. But big enough.

—— Male or.....female?

Dod looked at Wilf.

—— He's male all right.

He now thought Mister Wilf was a bit effeminate himself, come to that. The natty clothes and the cissy mannerisms and the elaborate gestures with the spotless hands. But surely a poof wouldn't keep a *real* dog like an alsatian? Anyway, if he was a poof so what. He had worked with them before. Usually very generous.

—— Well, we can't stand chatting here all day, can we lads? Work

to be done and I'm sure you boys are keen to get on with it.　I'll show
you where to put the goodies and then we must see that you boys have
a drink yourself before you leave.　On the house, of course.

　　But of course, thought Dod.

　　—— Thanks mate.

　　—— Think nothing of it.

And he minced off towards the hotel facade followed by the now-
silent Bongo.

　　——I didn't know you owned a dog, Dod.

　　—— Yes, he's a big beast.　A lovely animal.

　　—— What's he called?

　　—— Mister Bob's his name.

　　—— *Mister* Bob, Dod?

　　—— Everyone calls him that.　He's a big daft gentle creature.
All the kids like him.　He's a daft pal.　Wouldn't hurt a fly.　Not
like that big brute that runs and barks its head off at lorries.

　　—— His owner seems a quiet enough chap, Dod.　That Mister
Wilf.

Dod stuck a fag in his mouth, lit it and blew the smoke in a cynical
cloud into the air.

　　—— And pretty with it.

　　—— You don't think he's, well, peculiar?

　　—— Have a good look Sam.

And yards ahead of them now Wilf and Bongo were wending their
way to the entrance while occasionally Wilf would turn round and
gesticulate to them, showing them the cellar door where the beer was
to be dumped.

　　—— I wouldn't like to meet that buffer in the dark, Dod.

　　—— Who?　Mister Wilf?

　　—— No.　The dog I mean.

—— You can have them both for me.

But Dod was anxious to get the job over with so they could have a crack and a couple of jars and then he could have almost a whole day with Cathy. He could be back by three at the latest if he pushed himself, and when Mister Wilf returned, minus Bongo, Dod jumped out of his cabin.

—— In there is it?

—— Right first time.

—— Well, we'll just get on with it.

—— Don't you want a little hand, lads?

Dod shook his head.

—— No thanks, we'll manage.

The neat, natty, dapper, snappy hotel owner looked quizzically over both men then walked back.

—— Lets's get on with it Sam.

—— Coming Dod.

The work itself took about an hour and when they had finished loading the beer into the hotel they were really ready for a drink. Mister Wilf came to see the job completed and congratulated them on a speedy and efficient workrate.

—— You certainly deserve a drink. Well, lads, tell you what I've done. There's a couple of crates of strong ale in the inner room at the top of these stairs. You're welcome to have it all if you want. It's been chilled and there are glasses and a round of sandwiches — made by my own fair hands — each. I can't say fairer than that.

—— That's decent of you Mister Wilf.

Sam agreed.

—— Thank you very much indeed.

—— Don't mention it.

They climbed upstairs and, lo and behold, there was the treat just as Mister Wilf had said. Two preliminary bottles of ale were bolted down rapidly for starters, and then the sandwiches were quickly demolished and serious drinking commenced.

—— I must say, Dod, that was damned decent of Mister Wilf to put up a spread like that.   Usually it's just a quick pint and bye bye see you again.

Dod was brooding.   Beer tended to bring out the brooder in him.

—— He's a brute.

—— Still thinking about that dog, Sam?

—— No.   Mister lah-de-dah clever-dick Wilf.   I can't stand people who can't take care of themselves and have to get a dog to look after them.   And then they don't look after the dogs, let them go on the rampage.   People are worse than dogs.   They have no idea how to look after dogs.   An alsatian isn't basically a vicious dog.   He's tough when he has to be, yes.   I'll grant you that.   But leave him alone and he'll leave you alone.

—— Yes, Dod, but what about those attacks on young kids you're always reading about in the papers?   What about those?   They're alsatians.   They can't be so gentle.

—— The fault of the owners, Sam.   The fault of the owners.   Not the dog.   Not trained properly, see?

Sam nodded dutifully, like a faithful man's-best-friendly dog.   He accepted that Dod had manifestly superior intellectual powers.   Accepted Dod's word as law on many matters.   And he respected Dod as a warrior, a man useful to have as a friend if there was any boxing going on in the local.   He opened another two bottles of beer and they got stuck into them.   They could both knock back a lot and they there getting mellow, though neither was drunk. Dod, in particular, was determined to stay sober enough to negotiate the journey home without incident.   He could not afford to let Cathy down, and had no desire to make another exhibition of himself on the road.

He talked to Sam about Cathy for a while and told Sam he really thought he'd marry her.   He, the old magician.   They talked about marriage and people they knew who had fouled up their marriages and couples who had stuck it out through thick and thin, Derby-and-Joaning their way through life. They jointly concluded that a broken marriage was the fault of the man, and that, furthermore, if he allowed it to happen he deserved all he got and usually got what he deserved. Serve him right. If a man wasn't man enough to keep a woman happy, then he deserved *the lot*. And more. And if a woman got out of hand you just put your foot down and that was that. They jointly cogitated and found their solution to marital problems a good one.

—— You know, Sam, I'm going to marry that girl, my girl Cathy, and I'm going to look after her. Really. No, don't laugh. I'm not going to let her down. I may not become a new man because a man is made the way he is. But I'm going to cut down smoking because it just buggers my chest and to hell with spending all your money on drink just so's you can piss it up against a wall.

A look of enlightenment came over Sam's face.

—— By crumps, Dod, I'll have to go to the bathroom before we make a move.

—— Christ, right. I'll need a pee too.

—— Tell you what, Dod, I'll go and find out where the bathroom is and then do it and then you can go. How's that?

—— That's fine Sam.

Dod watched Sam get up and sway ever so slightly as he did so. Then he watched him go up the next flight of stairs on his mission to find 'the bathroom' as he euphemistically put it. Dod opened another bottle. The last, he promised himself. A good drink, then a good pee, and then — home to Cathy. And perhaps a walk through the park with Mister Bob. Cathy would have looked after Mister Bob as only she could. Cathy and his mum were the only two individuals he trusted Mister Bob with, though with Cathy taking up most of his leisure time he didn't see too much of his mum these days.

He wondered, abstractedly, what would have happened if he had known Cathy when he was a teenager. Impossible, because she was a good bit younger than him. No, if he'd been a teenager and she'd been then as she is now. Understanding. Sympathetic. Not interested in condemnation. Would he still have done all those stupid things? He doubted it. That robbery, for instance. That was absurd. There had been six of them and Dod, the hard man, was elected to bump the attendant in the local cinema while the other boys held up the cashier. In the event Dod only had to give one menacing look at the attendant and he aquiesced with their wishes. They had taken the money and piled into a fast car. So fast that they were arrested within the half hour. Even if they had got away with it, a six-way split would only have given them ten quid each. Hardly worth it considering the risk. They got off with light sentences because of their youth and because no-one had been hurt. But it was a black mark on a man's record and prospective employers were sometimes suspicious. A tealeaf is a tealeaf after all. But, he told himself, since the army he had reformed to a large degree. A couple of fights. Then — *bang* — into his reverie came an hysterical screaming.

—— Dod! Help! Dod! Help! Dod! Help!

Dod took the beer bottle from his lips. Sam was calling. Dod was up the stairs like a shot following the anguished cries. It was coming from the room marked *GENTLEMEN*. He pushed the door open and there, inside, on the floor, prostrate, upended, was Sam, pinned to the floor by a huge alsatian which had its front paws heavily on his neck. It must have been locked in there by its owner, only he hadn't told them that. And there was Sam, answering the dog's growls with his own invective.

—— By crumps, you buffer. You buffer you. By crumps.

Dod could only laugh. Even an aggressive alsatian could not provoke Sam into swearing. *By crumps, you buffer* it would be evermore. By the time Mister Wilf came in, in response to Sam's shouts, Dod was holding his sides and aching with laughter. *By crumps,* he was told, *you're a bit of a buffer yourself, Dod.*

On his way home Dod could hardly suppress his mirth. He kept seeing Sam spread out there murmuring *By crumps, you buffer* to a determined dog. And nothing had been harmed but Sam's pride. At least he had had his trousers on when attacked or the incident would have moved from the ridiculous to the realms of surrealistic sublimity. Dod thought how he would tell Cathy about it.

The beer was warm in his belly now and his head was perfectly clear. He was really enjoying the drive, just relaxing on the smooth roads. He looked in his side driving mirror: nothing behind him. Good. He looked at his personal mirror and was pleased with what he saw. There was a look of amused goodwill —charm even — that he hadn't noticed before. It had turned out too that the dog Bongo was well trained after all. Trained to trap and keep trapped but not to savage. And, in the company of the obsequiously apologetic Mister Wilf — 'Not in the loo, lads, what *would* my customers say!' — Dod had even patted Bongo with impunity. Fine beast. Yes, he would get on well with Mister Bob. Pity Bubblee's didn't allow dogs in the lorries. These dogs were both trained dogs with Mister Bob having the edge in etiquette. But of course.

His one regret was that the pubs would be closed by the time he got back. He would have liked a quick jar in the local with Cathy. But it couldn't be helped. They might buy a bottle of wine for the afternoon, then nip out later in the evening. The day was waiting to be made. Perhaps he could make her a meal in his new flat. He liked his new flat. Furnished and quite expensive, but he could afford it now and Cathy was adding personal touches that made him feel at home in it.

At three he swerved into the parking lot owned by Bubblee Brewers. Then he checked his wagon. Then he signed off. Two clear days ahead of him. Two day's leisure. With Cathy. He told the accountant about Sam and from the reaction the story was obviously going to go round all the drivers. Sam wouldn't be allowed to forget it. Dod would see to that. He grinned to himself as he repeated it again.

—— I swear that's what he said to that dog: *By crumps, you buffer.*

—— It had to be Sam.

—— Anyway, I'll be off now. See you.

—— See you in a couple of days, Dod. Enjoy your time off.

—— I will. See you.

—— Cheers.

—— So long.

Then Dod half ran, half skipped to the bus station, got on, cheerily greeted the fat conductress, and chuckled to himself all the way home. He jumped off with great aplomb at his usual stop and pelted, all excitement, up the stairs to the flat. Before he could get his keys out the door was opened. It was Cathy. Her eyes were red. She had been crying. She looked ghastly.

—— What the.......!

—— It's Mister Bob, Dod.

—— What?

—— He's......away.

Dod felt his body harden and his facial muscles snap to attention.

—— Cathy, what are you talking about?

Cathy looked at his face, white with rage. She was frightened. She had never seen him so angry or bewildered.

—— You must listen to me Dod. Please come in and sit

down.　Have a drink.　Calm down.

Dod gave her a look of disgust and he raised his voice alarmingly.

—— Just tell me, will you — now!

—— It wasn't my fault, Dod.　Honestly.　I took Mister Bob out for a walk yesterday morning, when you were away picking up your load.　We had just gone into the park to play, because he likes the park.　And there was this kid, a little boy, about eight.　And he, well, he tormented Mister Bob a bit, patted him at first, then pulled his tail, he should never have been in that park on his own, but then Mister Bob suddenly turned on him, it was horrible, Dod, he just started on the kid with his teeth, I tried to get him off but he snarled at me too, and we had to get the police and it took three coppers to get him off, they had to hit him with their batons, then they took him away and that's it, and I've been sitting here shaking ever since, and drinking whisky you know I don't usually drink whisky, but I've been so worried about what happened about the kid and that and about how you'd be when you heard about it.

By this time Cathy was sobbing helplessly and Dod tapped her shoulder and told her to sit down.　But he couldn't calm the storm that was within himself.　He could only drown it.　He poured himself a huge whisky.

—— Where did they take Mister Bob?

—— They didn't say.

—— Was it to the dogs home, was it?　So they can put him down?　Well if they do that someone'll suffer for it, no I don't mean you.

—— There was nothing I could do, Dod.

—— Why didn't you telegram me?

—— I was frightened, Dod.　Not just of what you'd think but of what you'd do.　I imagined you getting the news and going berserk on the road and doing something wrong or getting drunk and ruining things in your rage.

—— I loved that dog, Cathy.

This made her more penitent and the tears fairly splashed into the big glass of whisky cupped in her hand.

—— I know you did, Dod. I feel terrible, lousy, but what could I do?

—— Bloody stupid little kid. Tormenting a dog.

—— But Mister Bob used to love children.

—— Stupid little interfering brat of a kid.

—— Children don't know any better.

—— Was the kid badly hurt?

—— Shocked and cut and bleeding but the police got there in time and it was stopped in time.

—— So they took Mister Bob away for *that!*.

—— They had to. He might have done it again.

—— Not my Mister Bob, not with me.

—— But you can't always be with him Dod.

—— No.

He looked pensively at Cathy and shrugged his shoulders. The anger had given way to a feeling of helplessness. The thing had happened. What was there to be done but to go out and get pissed and that's what he'd do once he'd demolished all the booze there was in the house. That's what he'd do with his two free days. It was a bloody shame, he thought. A right bloody shame.

And drink he did. Swigging the whisky back with a vengeance and replenishing with a bottle of cheap red wine from the supermarket and having some cans of beer on top of that so that by the time he was ready to go to the pub he was already drunk.

—— Take the car Cathy.

She had a little Austin.

—— Dod, we can't. I can't drive after the whisky I've had. And you certainly can't.

—— Take the car woman. If you won't then I'll drive it myself. I've got a key remember.

She looked at him and knew he meant every word. She cursed the turn of events that had ended by him getting in a mood like this for he was unpredictible and rude and potentially violent when plastered. But she thought it would be safer if she drove, because then she could sober up in the pub and get home to bed safely so that perhaps the next day things wouldn't seem so totally black for him. Alcohol, the blackout drug, might lead to a dawn of blinding clarity. Might.

In the pub he was extremely aggressive, grimacing at people who inadvertently bumped into him, staring for solid minutes at innocent bystanders in for a half, banging into chairs and rebuking anyone who dared to comment on his clumsiness. He was in a very ugly mood and no-one, not even Cathy, was completely safe in the circumstances.

—— Try to forget it Dod.

He looked up at her accusingly. Then he showed his teeth again in that grimace of anger.

—— Forget Mister *Bob!* How could I ever forget Mister Bob. I loved that dog. I *loved* that dog.

Then he sprang up and shouted for silence in the bar.

—— Everyone shut up. Everyone shut up for two minutes. I want two minutes' silence for Mister Bob.

There was a hush throughout the bar. Nobody quite knew what to do and Dod had been so ostentatiously angry that night that nobody even knew whether or not it was some bizarre joke. Who *was* Mister Bob anyway? Yet the silence prevailed for about half a minute before the astonished barmanager broke it.

—— Right Dod, you've had your two minutes son. Now how about a bit of silence from you.

—— Are you insulting my dog?

—— Dod, I didn't even know you had a dog so how could I insult

your dog.   But you can't tell the customers to be silent.   This is a
public house remember.   And if you can't remember that then I'll
have to bar you.   And because of your behaviour this evening it
might mean barred for life.

There was an awkward moment of frozen conversation.   All eyes
were on Dod who had ben confronted on his own terms and who could
now either back down ignominiously or somehow vindicate himself.

Dod stared at the barmanager then suddenly broke into a broad
smile.

—— You're right chief.   I've been a bit of a bastard — oh, sorry
about the language.   Right, I'll buy you a drink and you and you and
you and you and you.

And he pointed to those he'd sinned against most egregiously and
they were relieved to accept the peace offering and feel that, after all,
the evening might prove to be a pleasant one.   Dod went to a table
with Cathy and, though he continued to drink heavily — a fact which
surprised the barmanager not one bit — he offered no more nuisance-
value.   Instead he brooded.   And when he brooded something was
being hatched in his nest of a mind.   And Cathy had her suspicions.

They were partly confirmed when they got out of the bar.

—— I want you to drive me somewhere, Cathy.

—— Yes, home.

True to her good intentions she had sobered herself up with an
excessive intake of tomato juice.

—— Not home, Cathy.   This is a test of your love.   This is when
you show yourself for what you are.   This is when you show me what
you're made of.

—— Sugar and spice not good enough?

He smiled and pinched her cheek, but there was malice in his eyes.

—— Either drive me or I drive myself.

—— Dod, you are dead drunk.   You cannot drive.

—— I can drive better that anyone else on Bubblee's fleet of lorries. I'm the top man. No bugger can outdrive me.

—— Well, let me drive you home.

And so they argued. But it was eventually no use. Nothing — except perhaps a pocketsize hydrogen bomb — could have stopped him on his nocturnal odyssey. He meant to have his way and she thought it best, finally, to go along with him rather than let him go it alone.

She got into the driving seat and he sat next to her. They drove to his directions. He'd had an appalling amount of whisky, she thought. But something was keeping him alert and it could only be the dog.

—— Is it Mister Bob, Dod?

—— He may still be saved.

She looked at him with horror.

—— Mister Bob was taken away. You understand that Dod. He did something wrong and they took him away. He's just a dog. Well, I don't mean it that way but dogs don't get second chances.

—— Turn right and stop.

She did as she was told and was amazed at the speed with which Dod got out of the car. Then she watched as he ran with amazing agility along the pavement in front of a high wall until he came to an iron gate. She drove closer and could see the sign at the door: CANINE CARE KENNELS. Of course! The dog home! Dod thought he could save Mister Bob. Christ!!!!!

She watched him clamber over the iron gate and go up to the caretaker's house which was inside the canine complex. Surely Dod could have rung for him from *outside* the gate, she thought. Instead he had already trespassed by climbing over a locked gate and going right up to the door of a private house at this time of night.

If that was bad the next thing was the worst thing that could possibly have happened. A startled fat man presented himself at the door and immediately Dod grabbed him by the collar and started squeezing his neck.

—— Where's Mister Bob?

Now whether the man knew what or who Mister Bob was, he was in no position to answer.   He struggled to speak but so tight was Dod's grip that he could only gasp for air.

—— Where's Mister Bob?

The man managed to get some of the fingers away from his windpipe and groaned for air.

—— I don't know what you mean.   Who is Mister Bob?

—— A big alsatian and if you've killed him I'll murder you.

—— No alsatians have been put to sleep this year.   None.

—— Liar!   Tell me where he is or I'll.....

But Cathy had looked up from the scene and through a bedroom window could see an anxious woman watching the ongoings.   The wife.   But of course.   And, naturally, they would have a phone.

—— Dod, his wife's upstairs, she's phoned for the police!

Dod was instantly silent, and then instinct took over.   He pushed the man back so hard he fell on his own doorstep and then he hurtled towards the iron gate.   Once over that he belted towards Cathy's car and, with her some yards behind him, got into the driving seat.   Then he started up and slammed down with his feet.

They got about a mile before the police cars began to close on them.   And by that time Dod was in no mood to submit quietly.

BLACK HOLE

Nerwin Higgins wondered how he had ever been talked into going on this mission.   Here he was, a space veteran at 28, undertaking the most dangerous flight of all when he could be at home, on Mother Earth, resting comfortably on his back-pay and his laurels.   He must have gone space-crazy, he told himself.   That was the only explanation.

He remembered, all too vividly, the first he heard about the flight.   He had been ready to set out on a simple earth-bound flight to what the brochures described as a holiday paradise in Africa.   He was well-known, wealthy and still wet about the ears.   His whole life had been dedicated to service to Space Control and he had decided that it was about time he embarked on what would be a normal life: wine, women and song.   He would, at last, break away from the gravitational pull of Space Control.

Then the videophone had gonged and there was the reassuring, well-worn, weatherbeaten face of his boss, Doctor Goldberg, speaking in the friendliest of tones.   At first Nerwin thought the good Doctor merely wished to send him away happy on his holiday.   But that thought was quickly rejected when the Doctor's face became deadly serious, the voice firm.

'Commander Higgins — *Nerwin*.   I want you to volunteer for a most astonishing mission, one that will ensure your immortality.' That sounded ominous for a start, Nerwin thought, mentally preparing

112

himself for a diplomatic refusal. 'This is without doubt the greatest sacrifice we have asked from anyone in Space Control.' *Sacrifice:* Nerwin was sure this was some sort of suicide mission. 'Come and see me at headquarters in two days and I promise you something you will never forget.'

Nerwin braced himself for his firm '*No*' but the face on the videophone faded out and the voice was replaced by a low humming noise. Two days — that meant no holiday. Two days — that meant worry and tension over some undefined task. Two days spent brooding at home when he could have been living it up for the first time in his life, at his holiday paradise. Yes, he thought, he was well trained by Space Control. He could not say 'No' to his master's voice.

When Nerwin finally came face to face with Doctor Goldberg he was unprepared, even after two days' frenzied meditation, for the nature of the mission. It was all so simple, explained Doctor Goldberg: 'What we went you to do, Nerwin, is to take a spacecraft close enough to a collapsing star to get photographs of a Black Hole.' Nerwin began to shake his head violently. The Doctor had to be joking. Nothing like this, so far as Nerwin knew, had been contemplated let alone proposed.

'There is nothing to worry about,' Goldberg continued. 'You can approach the gravitational radius of the collapsing star without being sucked in. You will have X-ray film equipment to penetrate the plasma clouds photographically but, remember, the actual process of collapse into a Black Hole takes less then a second, so be alert. Take two weeks holiday, report back for intensive training, and you'll be ready in two months. You are fit and experienced. That's why you have been chosen.'

As he left Space Control in a daze, Nerwin wondered how the Doctor had jumped from a request to volunteer to congratulations on being chosen, but he soon became lost in speculation about the mission itself. That bit about approaching the Black Hole without being sucked in sounded most unconvincing.   How could the Doctor know for sure?   Astrophysically it might be possible in theory, but human error could not be discounted, and Nerwin was beginning to feel he personified human error.

The holiday passed in a blink, and, anyway, Nerwin was well screened from wine, women and song.   Then came the training which consisted in revisions in superluminous flight and a crash course in X-ray photography.   Then he was off, after a reassuring handshake from Doctor Goldberg.   'You'll be immortal,' the Doctor had told him for the umpteenth time.

That second — in which the star collapsed and opted out of the observable universe — was the most astonishing in Nerwin's life. Through his X-ray viewfinder he could see a massive star (a white 'dwarf' in name only) instantly reduce itself to an intense crimson pinpoint, then there was a glorious halo in space, and then next to nothing.   And then Nerwin was shocked into movement.

For he felt his ship totter and then bullet towards the direction of the new nothingness in space.   He felt as though he were falling down a bottomless pit and the feeling of falling lasted, he would have calculated, about one hour in earth time.   The first thing he saw, on his ship's videophone, was the face of Dr. Goldberg.   Or what looked like the Doctor.

'Congratulations, Nerwin.   Well done.   You are the first man to come through to our anti-universe.   We are the positive of your cosmic negative.   I am, well, let's say, the positive of the Goldberg you know.   We have established radio contact with your universe but we had to see if a physical man could get through to the other side.   And you have, my boy, you have.'

'But why me?' Nerwin asked, even though he found the whole situation like a dream.

'Well, Nerwin, things at this stage are rather delicate but I assure you this anti-universe is what your flawed one could be.   To put it in terms of your crude theology — the Black Hole is, well, a kind of tunnel to Eden, to Paradise.   Whereas in your universe everything is imperfect, here we have cultivated the good and eliminated the bad.   What we had to do was to establish a physical link between the two universes.'

'But why me?' Nerwin demanded this time.

'Well, you, or your positive, exist here too, but in a, well, perfected state.   In other words you have freedom, happiness and your own woman — what you would call a wife.   We are not sure of the biological and sexual implications of this breakthrough, so we picked you to make the first flight because you were the only virgin employed by Space Control.   And now, Nerwin, come and meet your other self.'

THE VEGETABLE

THE VEGETABLE

The hospital was four miles from Helen's small rented flat so she had to be up at five in the morning when it was her early shift. This morning was a brutally cold one in April, the wind rattling her badly fitting windowframes. She shivered at the prospect of getting up for another day's work. Not because of the cold. Not because she had worked for seven years in the hospital. No. It was because of The Vegetable. The ubiquitous *IT*. She was depressed at the nature of her work, nursemaid to The Vegetable. She despised The Vegetable.

She had known, from the start, that the hospital was in the nature of a special institution for the study of the hopeless. It kept alive the bodies of people — 'things' — who could not exist outside its white-painted walls. She had known this, yes. But she had not been prepared for The Vegetable. *IT* did nothing. Some of the 'things' talked, mumbled, smiled, showed appreciation. Not The Vegetable. She realised, with a convulsive shudder, that most of her life was spent in the company of *IT*. She worked with *IT* and, away from work, thought of little else but *IT*.

Another day with The Vegetable. She slammed off the white alarm clock and mechanically began the process of preparing herself for the day's stint. She was an attractive woman of twenty-seven but she did not care any longer about her attractiveness. Her hair was straggly and prematurely grey at the sides. Her complexion was hospital-white. Her body was listless. She reasoned that, anyway, most of the patients in the hospital were in no position to notice the physical appearance of the nurses. And as for The Vegetable — *IT* wouldn't know. If *IT* had a mind she, Helen, would never enter into it. *IT* just existed and had to be looked after. That was what she was paid for.

Helen had a quick breakfast of slightly-burned bacon and had time to drink two cups of strong black coffee before she went to the bus stop. At least that was one thing to be said for working in a hospital: there was always a bus stop near it. She often asked herself why anyone bothered to visit the patients inside the hospital. Few of them could communicate, fewer still could communicate in a coherent fashion. They were a distressing sight. However, it was a job. The bus came and she nodded to the driver as she put her money in the ticket machine.

—— It's a cold morning.

Helen rubbed her hands to show she agreed with the driver and sat down on the nearest seat. The seat was cold. No one else had sat on it that morning. There were only two other people on the bus. She saw them every day she was on early shift. One, a small weedy man, worked in a hotel at something or other. So she had gathered over the years. The other, an elderly woman, cleaned offices. They exchanged observations on the coldness and retreated inside their particular silences.

Through the window Helen could see tall dark stone tenements sharp against the white early morning sky. It was only when the bus got nearer to the hospital that open spaces and trees and flowers came into their own. She liked the garden surrounding the hospital with its riot of colour, but thought it was wasted on the patients. How could they appreciate beauty? How could *IT* even be aware of anything outside itself? Bill, the gardener, was pottering about in the grounds. They called him Bill the gardener but he was really part of the place. He did any odd job and had quarters in the hospital. He kept the place clean and helped out in the kitchen but, simple soul that he was, he liked working in the garden. And because he was good at that they let him look after the garden. Helen thought Bill a bit moronic and resented the fact that, because he was retiring in a few months, she would have to contribute towards a present for him. It wouldn't be much but she earned so little that any deduction would be noticed.

She had not always been so indifferent to her work. When she left school she had first worked in a florists making up bunches of flowers. Then it had bored her and she felt a compulsion to do something valuable. So she had taken a nursing course. She might have done well in this career, she felt, but for The Vegetable. *IT* was there when she arrived. *IT* had been there since its birth sixteen years ago. *IT* was a medical aberration. When *IT* had been born the doctors were puzzled at the total lack of any reaction. No sense of sight or sound or touch or anything. They decided to examine *IT*. At first they thought *IT* would live for a few months. But *IT* went right on living. *IT* was fed mechanically: intravenously supplied and then purged. Helen had to do that. She thought it would kill *IT*. No. She had spent her working life keeping *IT* alive.

Yet it was not a life. She had said that to Doctor Lewis, head of the hospital research team. What, she had asked him, was the point of keeping such a totally useless object going. Doctor Lewis had frowned. It was not for them, he had said, to decide on such matters. There was a research programme to be carried out and the continued existence of The Vegetable was essential to it.

When Helen was not looking after The Vegetable her friend Rose took charge. They saw each other at every changeover and that was about the only friendship Helen had in her life. She entered the room where The Vegetable was kept and nodded to Rose.

—— How's it going?

—— You must be joking. Same as ever.

—— Just asked. You never know your luck. *IT* might have died in the night and made the world a happier place.

—— *IT* is immortal.

——I'm afraid so.

They smiled sadly at each other and then Helen looked at The Vegetable. Yes, *IT* just sat there, propped up, and pointless as ever. Nothing could change for *IT*. Yet someday, sometime, it had to die. A death to something that had never lived.

To the outsider The Vegetable would have appeared perfectly normal, yet abnormally still. There were no physical deformities, nothing to indicate total inactivity. The Vegetable was male. *IT* looked like a healthy sixteen-year-old boy in a hypnotic trance. *IT* stared ahead yet registered nothing. That was the astonishing thing. Encephalographs had revealed nothing: there was no trace of cerebral activity. The doctors had conducted hundreds of experiments to see if they could artificially stimulate muscular movement. But there was nothing. Yet neither was there muscular atrophy. Although The Vegetable had been still for sixteen years *IT* had grown from infancy to the brink of adulthood. It was totally baffling. Helen wished The Vegetable had been less baffling, for then it would not be so valuable to science. It was only because *IT* was needed for research that *IT* got the full treatment.

Helen was ready to start her work.

—— You going home now, Rose?

—— No, I'm going to the Royal Ballet.

—— Oh, I'm just making conversation.

—— I know, Helen, it's just that.....

—— Working with *IT*.

—— Yes, that's it. Working with *IT*.

—— I'm thinking of packing it in.

—— Same here.

Rose had not worked with The Vegetable for as long as Helen had, yet the strain was showing on her too. It was not just the distasteful task of keeping *IT* alive.   Helen and Rose had gone out on double dates with young men and when they found out the nature of their work they usually expressed extreme nausea.   *What are nice girls like you two doing........*   And Rose and Helen could not answer.

Rose was about to go when Doctor Lewis came in.   He motioned to a row of chairs so the two nurses could sit down and he stood in front of them.

—— I want to talk to you.   Both of you.

They shuffled in their chairs.

—— It's nothing about the quality of your work.   Something quite different.   As you know we have been carrying out a research programme on this subject here and we have decided that our tests have reached a dead end.

Helen wondered why Doctor Lewis bothered to call *IT* 'this subject' when everyone else called *IT* 'The Vegetable'.   Still, she wanted to hear what he had to say.

—— Now, there is definitely nothing more we can learn about this subject as things stand.   To be perfectly frank, we have learned absolutely nothing about this subject after years of research.   We have decided to terminate phase one of our research programme.

Rose looked at Helen.   Helen looked at Doctor Lewis.

—— But, Doctor, what will happen to The....your subject?

—— We have decided to terminate phase one, I told you.

—— How terminate?

—— I don't think I need go into details.

Helen looked anxious.

—— I think you should, Doctor Lewis.   Rose and I have looked after The Vegetable for years......

—— There you are, Helen: The Vegetable.   That's how you think of this subject.   You and Rose have always had nothing but contempt for your charge.   You have complained and said how unpleasant the work was and so on. Well, the experiment is to be terminated and you will be assigned to new duties.

—— But what are you going to do with *IT*?

Rose reiterated Helen's urgent question. The doctor looked at both of them gravely and then, with a sigh, opened his arms in a gesture of resignation.

—— Very well. I suppose I owe it to you both. A considerable amount of money has gone into this subject and as we have learned nothing from this subject in its present state of ...call it suspended animation, we have decided to induce death and then do a thorough post mortem on tissues and inner organs and the like in the hope of finding some clue to solve this enigma.

Helen gasped.

—— Induce death?

—— Yes Helen.

—— You mean kill The Vegetable?

—— I mean induce death.....medically.

—— But you can't!

—— I'm afraid we must.

There was a silence. There was little more to say. Helen and Rose exchanged glances in their confusion. Doctor Lewis stood his ground, his mind clearly made up. Outside the April wind was shaking the trees and Bill the gardener was walking about looking at his flowers. Then suddenly there was a sound, there was a musical sound, there was a sound, a sound from nowhere on earth. And there were words, a beautiful melodious voice.

—— Please allow me to comment on this situation.

The words were coming from The Vegetable. Doctor Lewis, Helen and Rose slowly turned towards *IT*. None of them could believe it. But there it was. The Vegetable was speaking and The Vegetable was standing up. *IT* lifted itself gracefully, smiled, and then elegantly walked over to them. *IT* motioned that the doctor should sit beside his two nurses and then fixed the three of them with two brilliant eyes.

—— The time has come for me to speak. I have listened with considerable interest to what you had to say, Doctor Lewis, and I have decided that it would not suit my purposes to have this body destroyed. I have been amused by my brief stay here. You call me The Vegetable, you young ladies, and yet your conception of what constitutes life is limited and primitive. Like you, Doctor Lewis, I have been engaged on a research project. It was necessary for me to study you people at close quarters, and to do this I took an observation post inside a human body. I wanted to study the human physiology and also the reaction of humanity to something you could not understand. Your reaction has been to probe the brain, to carry out clumsy methods of pseudo-scientific investigation. Your human reaction has been repulsion rather than interest. I have been able to see the capacity you have for kindness and, more obviously, for cruelty. You kept The Vegetable alive out of selfishness, not philanthropy. You mutilate flora for decoration, you consume your fauna. That is unnecessary — as I could show you. But it would not be worth it. This, your life, is an aberration, a biological blunder, a mistake, a mutation. It is uniquely ugly. As a species, you are hideous.......

Outside, in the cold April wind, Bill the gardener heard a sweet voice speaking. It was one he had not heard before. No matter, he would go back to his quarters for a cup of tea, now that he had finished in the garden. As he walked back to his room he saw, through a window, two familiar young nurses and Doctor Lewis. They seemed spellbound though there was no one else in the room. They must have removed that poor young creature, he thought. Bill shrugged his shoulders and assumed the whole thing was beyond his understanding. He would have that cup of tea to keep out the cold then he would do some work on his cabbage patch. Yes, that was his way of life. He would leave the complicated things to those equipped to understand them.

YOU'D NEED TO BE A SAINT

Tom was the stupidest boy in the whole school. Everybody said so, especially his classmates. He was slow and silly, they said. Thick as two planks. If a trick was conceived, it was with Tom as victim. If a scapegoat was required, he instinctively obliged. It was so easy and so endlessly amusing to catch Tom that even his teachers tacitly condoned the playground persecution. And Tom didn't seem to mind.

Yet though his (slightly protruding) teeth gleamed out contentment, Tom often felt like hitting back. He didn't because he knew it would make things worse. But he felt like it, just the same. His trouble, he knew, was his idiotic slack-mouthed manner. If he asked a question in class a surge of visceral excitement would overcome him and in his anxiety to impress he would gush out a verbal mixture that never failed to amuse the class.

—— Which famous missionary discovered and named the Victoria Falls?

Tom's hand would wave like the last signal of a drowning man. His feet beat out an agitated tom-tom on the grainy wooden floor.

—— Yes Tom?

—— George Washington, sir! He went up the Zambezi, and he.....

The elaborate answer would dissolve in the waves of laughter, the teacher would smile, and Tom would sink in the confusion of words that swam in his head.   Naturally, this lesson was not lost on the teacher.   Henceforth, if the class was sullen or openly antagonistic he need only invite Tom to speak and a smug tittering serenity would be restored.   Thus, everyone used Tom.   Except Miss Montgomery.

She was a young pretty history teacher who had come to the school that winter and was working well towards her first Christmas break.   As she listened to the staffroom anecdotes about Tom she shuddered, dreading the day when professional cynicism would settle on her shoulders like chalk from a blackboard.

She took an idealistic interest in Tom.   And he adored her in his fashion.

Once a week, with Tom's class, she went round each pupil asking for his or her favourite character in history.   When they obliged she would supply factual material and this would form the basis of an informed, and informative, class discussion.   Up till now Tom had been blank on the subject, but she could sense his foot-tapping excitement and smiled.

—— Have you a favourite historical character now, Tom?

He had obviously given it some consideration.

—— Saint Joan, miss!   I saw her on television and everyone said she was stupid and wrong but she wasn't stupid and wrong at all.

Miss Montgomery nodded and spoke above the sniggering of the class.

—— You saw a play about her on television, Tom.   Yes, she was indeed brave and has always been one of my own favourites.

—— She even looked like you, Miss Montgomery.   But it's all right.   They burned her but they don't burn saints anymore.   Not today they don't.

Miss Montgomery could feel the blood rush to her cheeks.   She was blushing furiously and the whole class scrutinised her reaction.

They seemed to generate a collective menace. Tom, however, was elated because he was being allowed to finish his sentences for once. He was warming to his theme, blissfully, dogmatically ignorant.

— And when they burned her she didn't yell, Miss Montgomery. So a saint doesn't feel pain. A saint's tough. A saint could conquer everybody in this class. A saint could go right up to Big Harry and punch him right on the nose. You could......

—— That's enough Tom.

—— I'll bet you could. I'll bet you're not afraid of anyone. I'll bet you wouldn't let anyone......

—— SHUT UP!

Miss Montgomery felt her own shriek piercing her throat and the shrill sound of her hysterical command horrified her. She could not at first admit that in one period she had been reduced to this —reacting with verbal violence to one boy's innocent obsessions.

Tom swallowed hard and looked at his desk. The class, Big Harry and all, sneered and shook their heads at him. It was like a sea of bobbing heads all saying NO. There was coughing and conspicuous silence. When the bell came it was a blessed relief and Miss Montgomery hurried to the staffroom, glad to be away from the class.

When the other teachers joined her they asked her about her obvious distress. Eventually she admitted that she was ashamed at adding to the humiliation of Tom. No-one agreed with her. The depute head reassured her.

—— Look, in my opinion he shouldn't be here. But he is and we have to put up with him. If you give him special attention he just drones on and wastes the time of the brighter pupils. What he is is a natural clown, so use him. He can be a useful safety valve. He doesn't mind, I'm sure of that. He probably enjoys being in the centre of it.

Although she was not convinced by this, Miss Montgomery

gradually found herself using Tom as a safety valve just as she had been advised. Then as the approach of Christmas imposed its atmosphere on the school she gently mocked Tom, finding it lifted the stress and responsibility of trying to teach a large class.

—— What are you getting from Santa, Tom?

For once he looked really hurt.

—— There's no such person, don't you know!

—— Come on, Tom. How do *you* know?

—— Because my father told me. I asked him why I didn't ever get presents and he said because there's no bleeding Santa Claus and you don't bleeding well expect me to waste bleeding money on bleeding presents for you.

The class convulsed with laughter. It had to be Tom's best performance yet. But his teeth didn't glitter and they didn't gleam. He looked straight at Miss Montgomery and it was her turn to look downwards. She almost apologised — but stopped herself in time to save her reputation with the class.

—— Don't let me hear language like that again, Tom.

—— It's what my father said and you asked.

—— Well, let's forget it this time and talk about something else.

She became aware of a tremendous commotion in the back row. It was Harry, undisputed leader of the class. Physically huge for his age, and very bright.

—— What's going on there?

She could see a dark bit of paper being handed around.

—— It's something Tom did in art today, miss. It's his Christmas card. It's very good.

Tom spun round and his face betrayed a sudden terror inside him. He sprang towards Harry but Miss Montgomery, shouting her way through the class, got there before Tom did.

—— You shouldn't have done that, Harry. I put it in the

bucket. I don't want it. It was no good. You took it.

—— SIT DOWN TOM!

He looked at her with dismay and reluctantly returned to his seat.

—— Why would you want to throw away your Christmas card, Tom? I thought you all made them to take home.

And she looked at the folded sheet of dark brown paper. It was crudely crayoned, in a childish pictorial shorthand, but she knew from the hairstyle and the gown and chequered dress that it was a drawing of herself. She was tied to a stake and red and yellow flames were clawing into her, burning past her body and reaching for her face.

THE DAY OF THE GAEL

130

THE DAY OF THE GAEL

Dear Norbert,

Long time no hear. You must have settled in to the new house in the new country with the new wife by now so I expect you've been busy. I thought just a short note to tell you what's been happening in this country of ours. You've probably read something about it in the papers — about the elections and that —but you've no idea what it's really like. You wouldn't recognise the old town. If you remember, the day they introduced decimalisation was bad; and the day they introduced metrication was even worse, I can tell you. Can you imagine? A half-litre of beer, eh? Makes you feel like an idiot trying to change the habits of a lifetime. But the worst day of all, the very worst of the lot, was the day they introduced Gaelic. *They?* You might well ask, for they weren't the *them* who had brought in a decimal and metric system. They were a different lot. I don't know where they came from. I doubt if they knew where they came from. They just sort of appeared out of nowhere. Mind you, there was a lot of talk about Gaelic being our ancestral language and all that sort of thing. You know, you'd get these know-alls, these clever dicks or clever jocks, on the telly and they would tell us about our birthright. A lot of bastards if you ask me. They said that once upon a time we had our own culture and language and music and God knows what else. The gist of it was that before the battle of Culloden — you'll remember hearing about that at school, everyone has heard of that, when we got tanked by the English — well, before

Culloden a lot of folk in the Highlands spoke Gaelic. They went about speaking Gaelic and they fought for Prince Charlie (who'd never set foot in Scotland before the uprising and who got the hell out of it afterwards) and they got hammered. It was worse than being slaughtered at Hampden by the English. After this horrible defeat the English put the boot in: nobody was to wear tartan or play the bagpipes or speak Gaelic. That was the worst cut of all — to the folk in the Highlands and islands anyway. That's the theory.

You can well imagine that the folk who had spoken Gaelic all their lives were not chuffed by this. It shattered them. Absolutely stunned them. One day they were speaking Gaelic among themselves; the next day they were supposed suddenly to talk English. Talk proper. A bit of a liberty when you think about it. Anyway, all this was in the past and somehow they managed to talk English like natives. That, you would think, was the end of it. But no. After centuries the only folk left who could talk Gaelic were people on wee islands and students and professors at Edinburgh and Glasgow. Good luck to them, I say. Let them talk in whatever language suits them. Live and let live. This, as I say, went on for ages and nobody thought much about it. Or so it seemed. Then one day this lot got into power. The Gaelic Association of Scotland. GAS for short. That's what they called themselves: GAS. Sounds appropriate if you ask me, but it took on. Like I said, they got into power.

You may well ask how it happened. Well, there there was this economic crisis and you'll remember there was always one of those. But this was the worst of all time. The very worst. The pound was inflated like a bairn's balloon and it was costing a score a time to have a night out. A quiet night, mind you. Money wasn't worth the paper it was printed on. It was stretched, so elastic that it bounced. The people started looking for a saviour. In Scotland we had whisky and oil and they made — according to GAS — a marvellous economic mixture. Some people will believe anything, as you know, and most Scottish people bought this one. GAS started saying they and only they had the answer because they represented the glorious past of Scotland when people had their tartan and their bagpipes and their porridge and their malt whisky and — you've guessed — their own language.   GAS said this key to the past would open the door to the future.   They said we were the victims of linguistic imperialism because we spoke, not our native language, but something forced on us.   I don't know how much truth there is in all that — frankly it sounds like bullshit to me — but nevertheless that's what they said.   And they kept on saying it.   They stuck to their guns.   And because the people had nothing else to turn to they turned, increasingly, to GAS.

I remember the morning it happened.   I'd been watching the pundits on telly the night before and had a few jars and a good few nips and when I woke up I had a splitting headache.   I felt fragile, all a-tremble.   You know the feeling.   Your head is spinning and you're ready for lift-off.   I'd gone into a bad pillow-spin the night before after all the experts had predicted which way the election would go and I felt awful.   I remember thinking how I visited Bill when he took the cure and how they gave him a dose of aversion therapy.   This seemed stupid to me because the boozer knows, in advance, that the inevitable result of a large alcoholic intake is going to be the most appalling hangover.   If that's not natural aversion therapy I don't know what is and it's never put me off boozing.   Anyway, I was feeling pretty low (Bill's back on the bottle, by the way, he got pissed the day after his discharge) and rather sorry for myself and was making vows that I'd never get that tight again.   So I turned on the radio and there it was.   The result.   GAS had won all the parliamentary seats in Scotland.   Every one of them.   In the circumstances the Westminister government had to honour their promise to grant GAS the independence it wanted.   We were, so a GAS spokesman said, free at last.   We were our own masters.   We had won the greatest victory since Bannockburn (another of those ancient battles they're always rabbiting on about).

Well, I thought, that's that. Things will go on the same as before and we'll all have a bit of a celebration — anything for a celebration — and think things have changed but it'll all be the same. Things never change — that's what I always thought. It's been like this since I was a lad: the country's going to the dogs and all we do is bitch on and bark about it. Sleeping dogs lie; alert ones tell the truth sort of thing, but it makes no odds. So I listened as this bloke droned on and on and said there were going to be some changes made. Oh aye, I thought, we've heard that one before. Pull the other one, it's got bells — or haigs or johnnie walkers — on. Then he said it. As from midnight a week on Monday Gaelic would replace English as the official language of Scotland. You could have knocked me down with a feather duster. Gaelic the official language! I mean, I didn't know a word of the bleeding Gaelic tongue and they're going to try to make me speak it. Just like that! And after all their pious talk about how dreadful it was of the English to force-feed us with their lingo; and there they were about to do the same thing. An eye for an eye, an I for whatever the first-personal pronoun is in Gaelic. It made me want to vomit. Well, I vomited anyway. Whether it was the result of the night before or this crazy announcement I wouldn't care to say. All I know is I felt sick. And I was. Thank God I got to the bog in time.

The first couple of days, under GAS, were uneventful enough. Naturally people went on speaking English as they had done (in a manner of speaking) for centuries. I mean, when you went on a bus you asked for the foot of the walk and not the equivalent in Gaelic. But then the change was introduced just as they said it would be. It was madness. When you turned on the radio the sounds that came out were incomprehensible. By this I took them to be the Gaelic language. Television, too, was converted to GAS. I thought perhaps this was some plot by out-of-work Gaelic-speaking actors so they could monopolise all the jobs. Shops, too had to change. When you looked at a pound of sugar — sorry, a half-kilo, I'd forgotten we'd gone metric — you saw this weird writing on it and

134

you had to feel it to make sure it was sugar and not something unspeakably Gaelic. This caused absolute chaos, of course, because shop-assistants, like the rest of us, were not all clued up on Gaelic. It was what the English had done to the Gael but in reverse. It seemed to me that the only people fluent enough to live their lives by Gaelic were the officials of GAS. It was a great day for them and for those who taught Gaelic. They were suddenly wealthy. GAS was determined to force Gaelic down our throats. They were not going to introduce it slowly but abruptly so we had no choice but to learn it. This was their revolutionary argument. Speak Gaelic or be damned. Teachers in schools had to be taught it so they could teach it to the kids. Newspaper editors were obliged to purchase a whole new range of type so they could print their rags in the official language. All it did, I reckoned, was to provide jobs for the Gaelic boys.

The first practical result of all this was that a lot of people voted with their feet. They hopped over the border, emigrated to England. This was fine in the beginning but the English authorities soon decided to put a stop to this by controlling immigration. And GAS could not countenance losing their best people. So a Border Wall was erected and police policed it and we in Scotland had to get passports — in Gaelic of course. What else? It was as if the country had gone mad — and in a way it had. It had voted in a bunch of language-besotted maniacs who wanted everyone to march to their tune. And their tune was a long lamentable lament dug up from the past. They played this tune morning, noon and night. A pibroch, I think it was. The only thing I could see in its favour was that it was wordless. Otherwise it would have meant yet more Gaelic piped into our homes.

I'd always thought there was something funny-peculiar about our country. What other nation, for example, has a weed and an insect for its symbols? Well, this old bat from down south was suddenly our Leader and she combined our symbols in her fancy name:

Arachne Thistleweed.   I noticed that she didn't have that done over into Gaelic.   What was good for the geese wasn't good enough for this particular gander.   Arachne Thistleweed, that was her name. Or, as we we called her (but secretly) Spiderwoman.   She had been born and bred in London but educated in Scotland where she caught the Gaelic bug bad.   She studied Gaelic at Edinburgh University and was apparently a star at it.   She claimed she could spout it like a native.   Well, thousands wouldn't but I believed her.   I didn't have much choice, did I ?   Not being *au fait* with the language and all that.   Yes, she was the big fish in the Scottish pond suddenly with her Gaelic airs and graces.   She was the boss-woman and what she said had to go.   If you could understand what she said, that is.   And she said the whole country — the newly independent nation — had to talk Gaelic.   It would be good for us.   It would reciprocate the infamous Highland Clearances.   Only this time it would be the Lowland Clearance of Language.   English had to go.   English would be swept out of Scotland with the maximum fuss and the minumum efficiency.

It was after many moons of this nonsense, with people reeling from the great change, that I decided to do something about it.   I decided to get rid of Spiderwoman.   I was sick of seeing her on telly uttering meaningless words and I thought: right, one of us has to go and it's not going to be me.   OK, the people had voted her party in but they got more than they bargained for.   They got a human spider whose stick-thin legs were wrapped round the manhood of Scotland drawing the virility out of it.   We were all trapped in her far-from-subtle web.   She wasn't an evil woman, I suppose.   Just a bit round the bend.   We had been warned by the other parties but they had now cleared off to England as they saw no future in Scotland.   As I saw it the few thousand Gaelic-speaking Scots — and English imports like Arachne Thistleweed — were a ridiculous minority who were obviously in the wrong.   I saw no reason why they should continue to have things all their way.   Even Bruce's spider had to try, try and try again. Why should this white-haired harridan try only once and succeed beyond even her wildest dreams. Her dream: our nightmare. Mind you, she was always the cocky sort. Full of herself and there being nothing of her, her legs hanging down like two woodbines dangling from a packet.

I'd been keeping myself to myself, sort of lying low seeing if the wind would change. No chance of that with GAS in control of the situation. I saw the members of GAS would never change their collective mind, not as long as that mind was lodged in the frail figure of Arachne Thistleweed. She wasn't having any arguments. Her word was law. She was firmly in charge of those under her. She crawled all over them in argument, she entangled them in spidery arguments that played on their collective conscience of which she was the guardian. They should be ashamed of this and that — especially *that,* the fact we had accepted the English genocide of the eighteenth century. Those Clearances — them and Culloden — seemed a more burning issue to GAS than what was happening right here and now. Well, to hell with them, I thought. Definitely, quite definitely, Spiderwoman will have to go. That's what I thought.

I've never been a violent person, you know that Norbert. All right, the odd shouting match in a pub; the odd skirmish with the police for making a disturbance. But what Scot worth his malt hasn't done something like that? I mean, it's all part and parcel of belonging to a small nation. You've got to act big sometimes. I've always felt that if you don't feel a surge of irrational and vicarious pride when the Scottish foootball team does well then you're dead from the neck down. No balls. That's what I've always reckoned. So, thinking along these lines, I didn't want to go out and do in Miss Thistleweed, old Spiderwoman. Not at all. Maybe I was a bit under the weather at the time but I really felt I could dispose of her in a non-violent way. Sort of persuade her kind of thing if you know what I mean. Explain to her in no uncertain words (English words to boot) that the ordinary folk of Scotland were not willing to put up with all her nonsense.   After all, she was English and what bloody business was it of her's to be more ethnic than the rest of us.   She hasn't a drop of Scottish blood in her varicose veins and that was reason enough for me to depose her.   Yes, depose her.   That was the thing.   She was like a queen of Scots the way she strutted about telling us to do this and that — only we couldn't understand her.

Talk about strut!   She held marches every day in Princes Street, walking at the head of her would-be clan, pipes playing, kilts swaying in the cold wind that rushes up from the Waverley steps and plays havoc with your nether regions.   She would come out of the Caledonian Hotel — which she had purloined as her own personal headquarters — and march along to the old Royal High School where she held court and made her daft laws.   As her party held all the seats there was, of course, no opposition to her suggestions.   Her word was absolute.   The others were just yes-men.   Affirmative weeds. So I knew it was easy enought to get near her and make a scene.   I felt if I could expose her for the usurper she was then I was all right, Norbert.   OK my son, I thought.   This is it.   Such was my reasoning, old chum.

The day I chose for the confrontation was a Saturday.   There would be a big crowd lining Princes Streeet to gawp at Spiderwoman as she made her regal progress from one end of the street to the other.   A marmorial Sir Walter Scott looked down with disdain at the proceedings from his plinth though I've always thought he was responsible for a lot of the nonsense that is talked in Scotland.   The Blizzard of the North, that's what I call him for his powers of obfuscation.   The General Assembly, big and dark and dirty, hung on the skyline.   In the background you could hear trains going to and fro.   Mainly fro, though, as — since the Border Wall and the English immigation laws — trains going south were strictly monitored by kilted officials whose only qualification for office was their abritrary ability (well, it's a geographical accident) to speak Gaelic.   Yes, Princes Street looked fantastic with all the flowers out, a circus of colours. What a situation! Can you imagine it, Norbert. I've described one side of Princes Street (only it's not called that now but something Gaelic), the side you'll remember. The other side, the commercial side, had changed because the shops were obliged to translate their names into Gaelic and quite frankly the whole thing was like Sanskrit to me. A row of strange letters and shops with ordinary and extraordinary labels. I know we're supposed to be daft as a nation but we're not that daft!

I waited outside the Royal Scottish Academy at the Mound, standing on the steps. Inside there was an exhibition devoted to the Clearances — of course! — with little models showing crofts being burned and great horrible nasty Englishmen doing Nazi-type things to innocent Scots. The English were presented like a horde of serpents in the Eden that was Gaeldom. Me, I couldn't believe life in the Gaelic part of Scotland could have been that wonderful. But we were expected to accept the official version of our history. This is what it had come to.

So I waited and then, precisely at ten, I heard the pipes. A low guttural lament just sort of hanging in the air like musical smoke. It got up your nose and into your eyes and rattled your eardrums. Then I could see them coming. The great Arachne Thistleweed and her mournful men. Strutting along, all of them. To me it looked pathetic, not at all stirring. On they came in their bogus tartans and spurious tweeds. A bunch of right Bonnie Prince Charlies. It was the thick reddish line and the thin end of the wedge all in one go. They represented all that was daft since GAS had come into their own again. There they were, large as life and twice as tragic; the ones responsible for the madness. And the crowd just gaped at them. Watched them making their march of progress along Princes Street. I knew I had to do something. I knew in that great street in mine own romantic town (thank you, Sir Walter) among my ain folk I was destined to be something of a saviour. It was my moment of truth.

Just as the procession reached the Academy I rushed forward, vaulted over the tubular barrier, and rushed right up to Arachne Thistleweed.   I think I intended to strangle her, to throttle her, to shake the life out of her, but when I looked in her face with her goitrous eyes and her pencil-thin lips and her cheeks stitched with red veins and her tight little helmet of white hair — well I stopped.   I was transfixed.   Even transfigured.   A little smile played on the severe lines of her mouth.   Instinctively I went forward and kissed her. Yes, the shame of it!   I kissed her.   I embraced her.   The crowd erupted in cheers, there was a crescendo of bravos, and some of Spiderwoman's faithful retainers came forward and shook my hand and patted me on the back.   I was a hero.   I had seemingly gone out of my way to show my undying gratitude to this self-appointed saviour of our national heritage.   This English she-wolf in sheep-stealer's clothing.   She had been dignified by my Judas kiss.   I had betrayed myself, gone back on my dynamic resolution.   I was helpless, felt humiliated.   And yet I was a hero.   Arachne took charge of the situation.   My movements had been too quick to be caught by the cameras and the television crews so — talking in a very cultured English voice — she told me to do the whole thing again for the benefit of the nation.   Captured on film this would be seen as a great gesture, something inspiring.   It had never happened before.   I doubt if any man had ever wanted to kiss Arachne Thistleweed before.   Only a fool would have done anything so crass and, Christ, did I feel a fool!   I could have buried my head in the tarmac, so impotent and inadequate did I feel.   And there she was telling me to do the whole thing again.   I was to go back to the crowd and repeat my gesture.   Only more slowly this time so the spontaneity of it could be carefully recorded.

There are few depths a man cannot sink to if he really tries.   I lowered myself unhesitatingly.   I sheepishly walked back to the steps, I dramatically re-enacted the whole thing and again the crowd cheered and again I was congratulated on my wonderfully patriotic act.   I was the man of the moment, the hero of the hour, the symbol of the people's love for their leader.   I was instantly part of the GAS propaganda machine.   That photograph — I was almost going to write pornograph — of me kissing the hideous lips of Arachne Thistleweed was used on posters and newspapers and publicity handouts.   MY foolish face became almost as well known as old Spiderwoman's herself.   I became a valuable asset to the organisation.   I was Miss Thistleweed's, and by extension GAS's, official mascot.   The fact that I couldn't speak a word of Gaelic was the only thing going against me and the great lady herself decided to do something about that.   I was to have a top-priority crash-course in Gaelic so I could speak in my capacity of chief camp-follower.

So there it is, Norbert.   Every day now I have to go to the government language laboratory in the old Royal High School to learn Gaelic.   I have to listen to tapes and talk back to tapes and record my progress on tape.   And the whole thing is monstrous.   I'm trapped and I don't know what to do.   Can I try again?   Sometimes I feel I'm going round the twist, like all those tapes I see.   My chance to save my country failed, and I've become a parody of my former self.   But what can I do, Norbert, what can I do?   I'm at a loose end.   Please advise me.   I await your answer with interest.   Give my love to Maggie and be good.

Yours aye,
Jack.

MEMO FROM: *THE LEADER* (translated from the Gaelic)

I see our policy of censoring English-language mail is a sound one. This man has clearly succumbed to the strain of instant immortality. I want him treated for intensive mental strain and recommend he be kept in Room 5B and supervised until he recovers. His face is too much of an asset to us; were his ravings to become public property the consequences could be potentially disastrous. See that he is cured without delay and ensure, of course, that his Gaelic lessons go on.

(Signed) **Arachne Thistleweed**

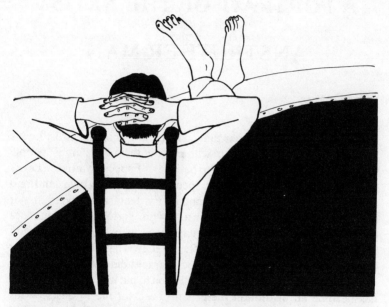

A PORTRAIT OF THE ARTIST
AS ANSTRUTHER MAN

A PORTRAIT OF THE ARTIST
AS
ANSTRUTHER MAN

When I think of the stories that could be told about the artist Lewis
MacBeth I realise the problem with most of them is that most people
today would find them difficult to believe.   Especially now.   Lewis
is famous, a prophet honoured spectacularly in his own land and
abroad.   His pictures are an obligatory feature of every major
collection.   Photographs of himself with various acquaintances
grace the pages of fashionable magazines whose connection with
matters artistic is normally nonexistent.   Lewis has made it big.   But
I knew him in the days when the social graces did not come easily to
him, when he could be pretty well relied on to put his foot in it.   As he
has become an institution there is no need for me to describe his
pictures.   They are ubiquitous, with their big curiously haunted
figures set against a dramatic seascape.   At least half a dozen books
have been devoted to his symbolism, his pictorial repertoire, his
thematic obsessions.   Good on Lewis.   No-one has deserved success more then he has.   In an age of visual charlatanism he has stood
out for the virtues of craftsmanship and dedication.   When I recall a
visit I once made with Lewis to East Germany I do so in no malicious
spirit of bringing him down to earth.   For that has always been his
element, as I intend to show.

The visit came about like this. Lewis and I were friendly with the composer Hamish Power. Now the introduction of another famous name makes this sound like an exercise in namedropping, which it isn't. We really did know Hamish well and he was the secretary of some Scottish/East German friendship society. Every year in Halle, Handel's birthplace, the East Germans hold a festival in honour of the town's most celebrated son. And the year I mean, in the early sixties, they decided to invite twenty Scottish composers over to mark the event with a display of friendship towards a place they supposed an oppressed country. One of the problems was that Scotland has hardly produced twenty composers in its entire history. There's William MacGibbon, there's Eugene D'Albert, there's Francis George Scott and of course there's Hamish Power. And that, as they say, is your lot. Hamish couldn't make it himself because of other commitments, and the sprinkling of Scottish composers he consulted were none too keen on making the journey behind the Iron Curtain. On a sudden inspirational impulse Hamish decided to save the situation by asking a Scottish writer and a Scottish painter to go instead. Cultural interdependence and all that. Lewis and myself, having nothing better to do at the time, accepted and were sent to Halle as Scotland's representatives in a great event. In theory it sounded a splendid idea. In practice it worked out in a funny old way.

At any rate Lewis and I fulfilled the first part of our duty. We duly arrived in Halle and a very attractive place it was. We were booked into a sumptuous double-room in a fine hotel and our first appearance at the ceremony round Handel's statue in the town square was ominous. First we were introduced to the crowd as the Scottish party and that bit of news was greeted with a burst of applause. Then an official asked to see us to work out an itinerary. While Lewis mingled, in his gregarious way, with the natives, it was explained to me that Lewis's attire was causing concern. This, remember, was in the early days of the Beatles and their sartorial impact was probably greater than their musical impact at that time. Lewis, always interested in being a man of his time, had grown a Beatle haircut and wore a skyblue collarless suit. At this stage it was the suit that offended the eyes of the people of Halle, so the official informed me. Diplomatically I explained that Lewis was well on his way to being recognised as a distinguished artist and in our country distinguished artists were permitted some eccentricities and, please, could he look on the skyblue suit as an aberration not a political insult. The official was not happy about this but there was very little he could do. Eventually he introduced me to a young man, Hans, who was to be our interpreter for the duration of our stay.

As neither Lewis nor myself could speak a word of German this was a most welcome development though it seemed that fluent English was the second language of all the Germans we met in Halle. Most of them could speak it with a more genuinely English sound than Lewis could. Lewis, as his biographers never tire of telling us, is from Anstruther, and despite his years down south he has never lost the breadth of his native accent. He still sounds as if he had stepped straight from a fishing boat in his native fishing village. So sometimes I had to interpret Lewis's Anstruther brand of east-coast Scots to Hans who then translated that into German for the benefit of puzzled listeners.

Our first encounter with, if not disaster, at least difficulty, came when Hans, as our official interpreter, took us to the little Handel museum in Halle. Actually there was no need for his interpretive skill for the curator of the museum, recognising us for the Scottish party, enthused about playing an English-language tape to guide us round the contents of the museum room-by-room. In the first room there was a series of reproductions and as we stood in front of the first one the disembodied voice began: 'You are looking at an engraving of the greatest of Handel's predecessors in Halle, Samuel Scheidt........' The remaining information was lost, submerged in the waves of laughter that came cascading from Lewis. Then he repeated the name to me with an infectious expression of sheer disbelief. Hans was at a loss to understand the great mirth provoked by the name of this illustrious innovator of organ music, and I tried to persuade him that the portrait of Scheidt reminded Lewis of our own Hamish Power and that that was somehow funny. Hans was a bit nonplussed but had no option but to accept the explanation. He grinned broadly as if trying to see the joke. In our room later that night, Lewis was still laughing.

I should explain that Lewis was totally uninterested in classical music. He liked a few popular singers and that was that. He had heard of Handel, naturally, but knew nothing by him apart from the Hallelujah Chorus. On our second night in Halle it was explained to us that we were being taken to a performance of the master's *Messiah.* Indeed we were and were ushered into the best seats in the house as befitted the Scottish party. We setttled down. The performance began. After about ten minutes Lewis began to ask me, in his loud Anstruther voice, when the thing ended. Already he was bored by the event and told me he strongly fancied a drink at the earliest opportunity. I whispered to him that there was a good while to go yet but he was adamant that at the first break he was going out for a bevvy. And we did just that, leaving Handel and The Lord behind us. Hans was aghast but made no direct comment on the *faux pas.* He told us, wearily round midnight that evening, that our next port of call would be Dresden. The Scottish party was to be shown off to the German Democratic Republicans. 'Great,' Lewis told him, 'yer a great wee boy.' Hans's grin had by now become a grimace.

So Dresden it was, for the Workers' Festival. On arrival we were picked up by a man who took us to a car that took us to the trade unionist in charge of the festival. This man could speak no English and everything he said was translated by Hans. At one point in the conversation Hans blushed the colour of the Red Flag. 'He says,' he said gesturing to the trade unionist, 'that Lewis's hair is too long. He has nothing against it personally but he feels that the workers might not like it and that Lewis might be in some danger in the streets.' The danger bit puzzled me, but it was true that Lewis's appearance in skyblue suit and Beatle haircut had reduced the crowds in Halle to hilarity. Lewis had always claimed it was me they found funny as I had prepared myself for the visit by having a short-cropped haircut. Now the truth was out. Hans looked at me. I looked at Lewis as if to say '*Well......*' It was up to him.

'Am no havin' ma hair cut off for naebody,' Lewis began. Hans explained patiently that it was either that or being sent home. I reasoned with Lewis as best I could and finally he relented. 'Ach, well aa right, but am just daein it for your sake mind.' The information was relayed back to the trade unionist who picked up a telephone on the desk before him and dialed a number and spoke. Within five minutes a barber had appeared and, without further ado, he began to put a cloth round Lewis's shoulders and cut his hair. Lewis succumbed to this injurious insult with muttered protests, even telling Hans to tell the beaming trade unionist to look at the bust of Karl Marx that adorned the room. The father of communism, as Lewis rightly observed, had not bothered with a haircut. Hans grimaced and did not bother with the translation. When the haircut was finished Lewis announced 'Well, I've come a cropper at last' and I laughed and Hans laughed and the barber laughed and the trade unionist managed a chuckle though he didn't know what we were laughing at. I thought to myself that the Germans had had their little revenge for what Churchill did to Dresden in the war.

The haircut did nothing to sharpen Lewis's sense of diplomacy. In fact he complained about it for several hours. His sense of grievance was intensified when he asked Hans to direct him to a shop where he could buy a shampoo. It proved an exceedingly difficult commodity to obtain and Lewis kept repeating 'What kindae a country is this anyway when ye cannae git a shampoo.' After some to-ing and fro-ing we tracked down a shop that sold shampoos and Lewis retired to the bathroom to emerge lobster-bright an hour later explaining that he had fallen asleep in the bath and was by now fed up with the German Democratic Republic.

Still the next day dawned and Lewis's spirits recovered when he learned that we were to be taken to the art gallery in Dresden. He knew there were some great paintings there and bought reproductions of many of them. He also startled Hans by telling him that he could draw as well as Holbein and paint as well as Giorgione. Hans turned to me with an astonished expression and I told him that Lewis was considered to be one of the finest young pictorial technicians in Britain. When we got back to our hotel room, however, one of the finest young pictorial technicians in Britain blotted his copybook by spreading out his reproductions on the bed then pinning them to the walls. 'You cannot deface the walls with pins, Lewis,' Hans protested. 'Well, ah'll use sellotape instead then,' Lewis responded and produced a roll of sticky tape. Hans sighed a terribly profound sigh and told Lewis this would be even worse. 'What the hell kin a boy dae in this place?' Lewis asked rhetorically. 'Please do not make yourself so conspicuous,' Hans suggested. Seeing that Lewis's temper was in the process of getting lost in East Germany, I told him it was just the difficulty of Anstruther Man adapting to a different cultural climate. 'Well, Anstruther Man's getting pretty fed up wi' this place,' he shouted.

Soon Lewis's natural exuberance returned, especially when we prepared to leave Dresden for our last stop, Berlin. On our final evening in Dresden Lewis surprised Hans and myself by telling us that tonight was his twentyfifth birthday. 'It's ma quarter-o-a-century the night an' by Christ am gauntae have a boozerama.' He got Hans to phone for a table for three at the best restaurant in Dresden then retired to smarten himself up for the big night. Since arriving in Dresden the skyblue suit had been exchanged for a more appropriate outfit comprising sports jacket and dark trousers. For the big night, though, the skyblue suit was donned again. I thought nothing of it but noted that Hans looked unhappy.   If he had a premonition it was a justified one.   When we approached the posh restaurant the doorman conferred with Hans in German.   Sadly Hans came to an elated Lewis and explained: 'He says that two of us can come in, Lewis, but not you, not in those clothes.'   'These claes,' Lewis yelled, 'these claes cost me a packet.   Ah've a good mind to stick one on him.'   Hans returned to the doorman.   I doubt if the translation was, on that occasion, a literal one.

The trials of Dresden faded into memory as we headed for Berlin.   Here we booked into the East German equivalent of a Hilton Hotel.   It was magnificent and Hans told us that once, on a journey to Berlin, he had tried to get into the hotel for a look around and had been refused entry.   This fascinated Lewis who, relating it to his rebuff in Dresden, opinionated that in some aspects East Germany was a dead loss.   He was only slightly deflated when Hans said the evening had been arranged round yet another official event.   We were to be taken to see the Berliner Ensemble performing Brecht's *Threepenny Opera*.   I knew this was to be the absolute pinnacle of our visit, but Lewis didn't register much appreciation.   'Och, ah suppose it'll be aa right' was his only comment.   Alas it wasn't.   It was the worst confrontation between the mentality of Anstruther Man and the ethics of East Germany.

Lewis, Hans and I were given a box to ourselves for the performance.   It was explained to us that from the same box the Soviet premier had once watched the Berliner Ensemble.   Enough said. We were privileged indeed.   On top of this the performance was being televised for live showing on East German screens.   Lewis, who had been extremely reluctant to sample most of the items on our cultural agenda, relaxed noticeably during the Brecht play.   Although it was in German the musical panache of the show communicated itself to him.   He sat back in his chair.   He obviously felt expansive, at home.   Then he took off one shoe, then another.   I hoped Hans wouldn't notice.   Then Lewis took off both his socks and placed his feet up on the edge of the box. Again I said nothing hoping the spectacle would pass unseen. It was too bad to last. Soon a forbidding figure beckoned us from the box and asked us to leave on account of Lewis's feet. 'Right,' fumed Lewis and loudly stormed out. Having no desire to linger I followed Lewis smartish and the three of us went to a bar where two of us got very drunk indeed. Lewis was horrified at the treatment meted out to him, a representative of Scotland. 'If that happened back hame,' he told the sober and suffering Hans 'naebody would have bothered; fancy gettin' the order o' the boot!' I said nothing. Hans must have had all his suppositions about capitalist decadence confirmed.

The two days after the theatrical disaster were free. Lewis and I spent most of the time shopping and drinking. Nothing untoward happened and the final Friday came to pass. In the morning we were taken to a lecture on the Berlin Wall and then to the wall itself. Lewis and I were so hungover that we hardly spoke during the whole affair. Before we got our train back to the west we were to have lunch with the minister in charge of the arts. A lady. We met her and, through Hans, Lewis told her he had vastly enjoyed his stay in the German Democratic Republic. She looked suitably pleased. Then from his briefcase Lewis produced a drawing which, he explained, he wanted to give to the government as a token of his appreciation. The thought was a good one as was the drawing. The only flaw in the whole thing was that it was a full-length drawing of a nude female model, pubic hair and all. The lady said nothing about the drawing, quickly finished her meal and left. All the time the drawing lay on the table for all to see. There was no question of Lewis deliberately trying to unsettle the lady. He had done his best. It was just that Anstruther Man had inadvertently blundered again.

At the station I was expecting some kind of reproach from Hans about the drawing which had now been placed into his hands. However he said he would see that it got to the appropriate authorities. Then Hans said to Lewis: 'Lewis, if you ever come again and have a meal with Frau' — and here he named the official — 'please do not push your plate away after eating then belch then say "That's better".' It was a mild rebuke from a young man who had done a difficult job rather well. Lewis looked at him and said with scorn: 'Aye, right ye are, but when I get back hame ah'll belch as much as I like. That's what democracy's aa aboot.'

We parted from Hans and on the train back Lewis confided to me, 'We'd be best no tae talk aboot thae things that happened, ye ken, the haircut and the play and that; it's no that ahm bothered, it's just that it'd look bad for East Germany and we had a smashin' time.' I nodded. And until today I've said nothing about the East German odyssey of Anstruther Man. Then, this morning, in the newspaper I noticed that a retrospective exhibition of Lewis's painting was to be taken on a tour of the communist countries, doubtless to show them the strong figurative tradition that flourished in Britain. And the artist was to tour with his work. And one of the venues was East Germany. Much as I enjoy travelling I'm glad that I've not been asked to be one of the Scottish party this time.

BROKEN OCTAVES

BROKEN OCTAVES

Bill Fisher played piano in the lounge of a pretentious hotel that squatted, with ugly concrete certainty, on the periphery of Edinburgh. The hotel was called The Native Land, a title that the owner, Mr. da Vinci, thought had immense class. Mr. da Vinci (he always insisted on the Mr.) had picked up the phrase at school when, over-sensitive about his Italian origins, he longed to be more Scottish than the Scots. One day a teacher read to the class from *The Lay of the Last Minstrel* by Sir Walter Scott (whose patriotic surname fascinated the young da Vinci) and eventually chanted the magic words:

> Breathes there the man, with soul so dead,
> Who never to himself hath said,
> This is my own, my native land!

At that moment Charles da Vinci had known he was home and had resolved to make a name for himself in Scotland. And he had. And that name was *The Native Land*. It was his place, he owned it lock stock and barrel.

To Bill Fisher *The Native Land* was a painful place to play piano. He had nothing at all against the ebullient Mr. da Vinci and indeed admired his simple patriotism and business acumen. Mr. da Vinci paid well for Bill's services and was a good employer, so everything was satisfactory on that score. What Bill objected to was the necessity of playing mindless cocktail music for hours on end while people less gifted than himself sat and made unspeakably loud noises by the application of food to mouths. ate noisily

154

Bill Fisher had begun life with a burning ambition to be a concert pianist and had studied music, first in his native Glasgow and then in London.   He had been told, however, that he simply would never attain that coalescence of profound artistry and supreme technical virtuosity needed by the performer with aspirations to international success.   Bill was sure he had the emotional equipment for he could be moved to tears by a Mahler song (especially one from *Kindertoten-lieder*) or by a Beethoven sonata.   Quite simply, he felt, his fingers had let him down: they could not translate his deepest emotions into the terms of the classical keyboard.

To look at Bill Fisher it would have been difficult to realise just how sensitive and introspective and vulnerable he was.   He was very tall, had an unfashionably close-cropped haircut, and his prominent nose and jutting chin suggested strength of character.   Yet he was forever analysing himself, forever formulating theories as to why he wasn't better at such-and-such.   He felt he knew why he was not going to be a great classical pianist: he was not cut out to be one.   He had come from a working class part of Glasgow and had, as a child, been embarrassed by his parents' insistence on sending him to piano lessons.   Classical music was synonymous with cissification in Glasgow, and Bill frequently got hell because it was assumed he thought he was a cut above the others.   How then, Bill reasoned, could he have properly absorbed the European classical tradition in those circumstances?   It was temperamentally alien to him.   He had been conditioned on the streets to distrust it, to see it as an integral part of a life of privilege.   He was not environmentally moulded for classical music and though he had tried manfully to master the alien tradition he had failed.   So be it: it was not the end of the world.

Although technically Bill Fisher was not in the first rank of pianists, no one could deny his qualities.   He had a lightness of touch and a fluency that was delightful to the ear.   Bill remembered that the only way he had been able to use his gift to advantage as a child was when he impressed his friends by 'jazzing up' well-known tunes.   What he

155

did was give a staccato rhythm and strong left-hand bass to a melody and the other kids responded with smiles and laughter and applause. That was the tradition Bill Fisher belonged to: the tradition of music made palatable to his own kind of people.   In modern terms Bill felt that only jazz was capable of communicating on a deep level with his people.   Classical music inhibited them; pop music was far too ephemeral and undemanding to do them any good.

In his enthusiasm Bill made a thorough study of the modern jazz that developed on the American east coast after the manner of Charlie Parker, the great saxophonist.   Bill found that Parker had been succeeded by jazz musicians intent on experimentation who, in their ignorance, thought they were being musically adventurous when they were only duplicating harmonic effects Schoenberg had made commonplace in the 1920s.   Though greatly gifted, many of these jazz musicians were musically illiterate and theoretically primitive.   Bill Fisher felt he was in a unique position to graft his academic knowledge of musical structure and harmony onto the vitality of jazz.   The result would appeal to the public without treating them as musical cretins.   The music would touch the heart, but also tax the mind.

Unfortunately for Bill, no one was particularly interested in his advocacy of a completely new kind of modern jazz.   The few clubs that wanted a jazz pianist had a conventional one.   Bill left college without thinking much about a career but an additional factor entered his life, and changed it.   One night, in London, he met Liz outside a cinema.   It was pouring with rain and they were sort of washed together by the weather.   They watched the film together, held hands, and things developed from there.   Liz was a real lassie from Lancashire (Bill wrote pseudo-Beethovian variations on the song for her) and had come to London as a typist.   They felt life would be better together and so they got married.   Henceforth Bill urgently needed a job.

Rather than teach, he decided to make music of some sort.   He got a job playing electric organ with an unsuccessful pop group and had to tour with them in all kinds of weather for a pittance. Apart from being musically frustrating it was not fair on Liz who had now become pregnant. What Bill needed was a steady, not a nomadic, job, and thus he had come to Charles da Vinci, owner of *The Native Land*, who had advertised for a pianist for his hotel. Tremendously impressed by Bill's qualifications, Mr. da Vinci was sure he had hired a genius. Nevertheless he insisted that Bill, when on duty, must play inoffensive cocktail music. It had to be quieter than the chatter of the paying guests. 'As long as it is tasteful, Bill,' Mr. da Vinci had told him, 'then it will do. It must be like the food I serve — tasteful. Your music, though, should be an aid to digestion not a meal in itself. It is background music.' And Bill had nodded and done what he was told because the money da Vinci gave him paid the rent and paid for Liz and for the baby.

Bill lasted a year, a year of smiling at the customers and tinkling out muzak for them. One night, in response to a drunken customer, Bill had performed in his own style. He produced a version of 'Over the Rainbow' that retained the basic melody but subjected it to an intricate restructuring and many melodic variations. The customers applauded and a good time was had by all except Charles da Vinci. 'No Bill,' he had said gently, 'I don't want that kind of music. I want a man sitting there playing soft music. The word is tasteful: *The Native Place* is my creation, my work of art if you like. Every detail must be as I want it.'

Bill had lost his temper and insulted Mr. da Vinci. 'A work of art is beautiful,' he had told his employer, 'not tatty like this place. And this place is tatty and shabby and cheap because it is made in your image, MISTER da Vinci.' But Mr. da Vinci understood. He told Bill he realised he was worried what with a wife and a young baby and the rest of it. He was tired but would feel better the next day. There would be no hard feelings. Bill had had enough, though. He handed in his notice that night. Mr. da Vinci was very sorry to lose him and wished him well.

4
Jazz
trio

When he got home that night Bill told his wife of his decision to do something about his real ambitions. He would make jazz like it had never been made before. Liz had never really shared his love of jazz but pretended to, for his sake. She went along with his plans and said it would be all right as long as they had enough money for the child. She had never been rich, so a little more poverty would be no novelty. Thus the Bill Fisher Classical Jazz Trio was born; or, rather, still-born. Bill got a couple of mates — both talented enough — to join him, and they tried to make some impression on Scotland. They got no further than the Universities and the atmosphere there was hardly inducive to a great innovation in music. The students drank and joked as they listened to the music and Bill found himself drinking and joking himself to cover up the pain of failure that engulfed him after those sessions. They were not going to set the heather on fire.

5
Jazz
solo

There is little else to tell. Bill Fisher's group broke up but Bill and Liz and the kid went to London where he hoped to make a solo breakthrough. In London Bill became a jazz club bore. He drank so much that he made a fool of himself whenever anyone was persuaded to let him sit in during a session. His continued assertion that he was about to leave for Harlem to reshape jazz there became a running joke. He was good for a laugh for a short while but quickly became unbearable and was liable to turn nasty with drink.

6.
dead

After a year in London no one wanted to know him and one day Liz found him dead. He had drink on his breath, pills in his body, and his face in the bath.

Dear Mrs Fisher,

        Ever since I saw you at the funeral I've wanted to write but up to now I couldn't.   I've done nothing but cry since it happened and my mum has been in looking after the baby.   I felt I had to write because people can be so cruel and when I saw you at the funeral I felt you felt I was to blame in some way.   I'm sure no one is to blame.   Bill was so clever, as you know, but he could never stop dreaming and even his friends from his college days said he dreamed too much.   They said he could have been a great piano teacher and that with his background, being from Scotland and so on, he couldn't really have jazz in his blood.   He could have done so well if he had left his dreams alone but something drove him on, I don't know what it was.   He was so kind and quiet sometimes, then — he'd have another dream, he was going to do this and that.   But it never came to anything, just heartbreak for those who loved him.   I loved him and I know you and Mr Fisher did, he often told me how much he loved you.   Still, he wouldn't listen to anyone when he had an idea.   He would have made a lovely father for little Art (as Bill called him) but we've got our memories.

All my love,

Liz.

PS.   I thought what Mr. da Vinci, the man Bill worked for, said at the funeral was so true.   He said to me that it all started to go wrong when Bill left his job at Mr. da Vinci's hotel.   It was a good hotel and he got good money and we were all so happy when he was there.   I'll write again soon, must dash.

THE EARLY LIFE
OF
DOLLY SILVER

One: Paradise Regained

Beware, O Man — for knowledge must to thee
Like the great flood to Egypt, ever be.
Shelley, 'To The Nile'

The Cerebral Express slid sleekly into Mainline Station. Dolly Silver, high-heeled and high-breasted, strode elegantly onto the platform surrounded by her faithful followers.

'The revolution is complete, comrades,' she declared to an outburst of fanatical applause. The crowd, controlled by beautiful women-guards, jostled to get near Dolly. The revolution was complete.

The revolution was complete. How it got completed is a short story. To appreciate the genesis of it all we have to dissolve back a bit, for once Dolly was only an artschool model, though she was, to be sure, one of the very best.

Two: Horses for Courses

> Take her up tenderly
> Lift her with care;
> Fashioned so slenderly,
> Young, and so fair!
> *Thomas Hood, 'The Bridge of Sighs'*

The artschool was a shitty-looking building, custom-built for mediocrity. It was off-colour and the main door was off-centre. The whole thing looked like a deliberate mistake, an architectural plan that had been botched in the first and final stage. The students who came to it knew they were, at best, second-best. They arrived in little conspiratorial groups, keeping close together. They talked, in stage whispers, of what they would do with the rest of their lives. Always they were well aware they would never amount to much. The air was thick with the promise of failure.

All the students wore uniforms as drearily conformist as the old school uniforms they thought they had discarded. Jeans and long shapeless sweaters for the birds; jeans and old macs for the blokes.

Three: The Road To Damascus

O Woman! in our hours of ease,
Uncertain, coy, and hard to please,
And variable as the shade.
                    Walter Scott, 'Marmion'

Dolly Silver was twenty when she first came to the artschool.   That was not *the* beginning.   Since leaving school (non-artschool) she had drifted through a variety of jobs.   She started as a typist but couldn't really type.   Then she worked in a canteen but couldn't really cook.   And so on until you get the picture.   One night in the boozer Dolly was cogitating over a glass of low-calorie Fizz.   A guy, half-pissed on port and lemonade, looked her over and chatted her up.   The gist of his drivel was how fantastic she looked.

'Dolly, you're a fantastic bird.   You look fantastic.'

Dolly brushed him off, like a loose shoulder-hair, after accepting a few glasses of Fizz.   When she got home, on her ownsome, she thought about his words and they struck her with the full force of a revelation.   It was a Pauline moment.   She *was* a fantastic bird.   It had taken her a while to discover this.   She was, mentally, a late developer.

She stripped off and looked at herself in the cheval-glass.   She weighed her ample tits in her elegant hands.   Perfect.   She turned sideways and glanced over her shoulder at her undulating shape.   Wonderful.   She looked full-frontally at her form.   In and out like an hour-glass.   Like a sexual metaphor.   She decided she could easily cash in on her looks though she was not the mercenary kind.   That face, that figure — those were her firm and solid assets.

Four: Sugar And Spice

Two men look out through the same bars:
One sees the mud, and one the stars.
Frederick Langbridge, 'A Cluster of Quiet Thoughts'

Having turned nineteen, Dolly applied for a job as a gogo dancer in the same pub where the prophetic drunk had propositioned her. The job was hers for the asking. She was an instant wow with the customers. She dressed in a shimmering outfit that sparkled as she put her flesh about. The bra was built like a solid silver structure and her breasts brimmed over. The panties were soft and clinging, made to show her secondary cleavage. Dolly wiggled about on stage in her silver costume and basked in the appreciation the customers gave her. They ogled, she performed. There wasn't a soft prick in the place when Dolly danced.

Many of the boozers tried to take her home. Always she refused. She valued her body. Put a premium on it. She did not fancy penetration by a man high on alcohol and low on energy. She would keep herself for the right man. If he came along, fine. If not, just as fine. Dolly could wait. She could take it or leave it. She wasn't desperate.

Five: The Beaver Cometh

They need their pious exercises less
Than schooling in the Pleasures.
George Meredith, 'A Certain People'

The gogo job lasted for more than a year.   Then Dolly retired.   She had had enough.   Having discovered the power her body exerted over men she felt she might do something more worthwhile than titillating them.   One evening a bearded weed had approached her and talked about art.   It was almost the same old story.   Almost but not quite.

He told her she had classical perfection of form and that her body should be a thing of beauty rather than an object of lust.   Told her so in so many words.

'Dolly,' he spluttered, 'your body is a thing of beauty.   You should be painted.'

'Naw,' our heroine protested, 'I dinnae like body-paint, dinnae fancy it.   Mabel uses it and she ends up havin tae scrub herself.   Aw-fae.'

'No, no, no, no, no, no,' the beaver persisted, 'I don't mean that.   I don't mean that at all.   That's not what I mean.'

'So,' shrilled Dolly, 'what are ye on aboot?'

'Well, I don't want to boast,' boasted the beaver, 'but I'm a painter.   I'd like to paint you.   I mean I'd like to put you on the canvas.'

'Are you trying tae make me, Big Boy?' Dolly enquired in a phrase borrowed from Mabel.   As soon as she said it she disliked the sound of it.

'No, no, no, no, no, no,' protested the beaver.   'I'm an artist.   I appreciate your beauty.   Be my model.'

'You want yer heid examined,' Dolly retorted and wiggled off to the loo to change back into her civvies.

When she got home there was another session in front of the cheval-glass. Yes, that turd had been right. She *was* fit for higher things. Higher things than gogo dancing. She would change her life.

Six: Pretty as A Picture

Woman! when I behold thee flippant, vain,
Inconstant, childish, proud, and full of fancies.
Keats, 'Woman! When I behold Thee'

Although it meant a drastic drop in salary Dolly changed her job.   Next time she saw the bearded Romeo she asked him about modelling.   She did not want to model for one man but for all mankind.   The result of this conversation was Dolly's first visit to the artschool.   The Principal took an instant shine to her.   Yes, the artschool would be delighted to employ her on a probationary basis.   She signed on for posterity.

Seven: Art For Art's Sake

Who teaches the mind its proper face to scan,
And hold the faithful mirror up to man.
Robert Lloyd, 'The Actor'

Worth a few bob by now (from the profits on her dancing) Dolly began work in the artschool. Her work was simplicity itself. She stripped off in a special room then walked, wrapped in a cloak, to another room. There she stood, in her altogether, near a radiator. Her magnificent feet rested on wooden floorboards. There the students painted her. Painted her with a passion. Some of the male students found it difficult to concentrate with Dolly's provocative presence before them. They would wriggle about uncomfortably and ask permission to leave the room from time to time. Dolly wondered at their behavior. But then, she had never known artists before.

For several months Dolly stuck at the modelling. She was waiting for the moment when she could recognise herself in the paintings the students laboured on. The first ones she saw were ghastly but, she realised, the poor wee souls hadn't learned to draw yet. The female students portrayed her like a caricature of an Amazon. The male students seemed to concentrate entirely on the challenge of her epic bust. She would give them another chance. They were beginners. She could see that. Once they had learned to draw, their painting would tell a different story.

Month after month, though, the story was the same. She came, they saw, she blanched at the result. She came to the conclusion that these students were a bunch of no-hopers. The only talented artist in the place, so far as Dolly could judge from informed gossip, was the Principal. He was a fine figure of a middle-aged man, silver-haired and distinguished. He worked away in a private room. Dolly liked the look of him. She thought him terribly nice.

Eight: The Apple Of His Eye

Dull sublunary lovers love
(Whose soul is sense) cannot admit
Absence, because it doth remove
Those things which elemented it.
John Donne, 'A Valediction Forbidding Mourning'

One day the Principal summoned her to his private office. He asked her to sit down. She did. He offered a gold-tipped cigarette. She declined. He lit up. He inhaled. He blew smoke into the room. He looked grave.

'Dolly,' he began, 'I hope you are happy here.'

'I'm no complainin,' said Dolly, 'ye ken, it's no sae bad.'

'I feel you are wasted on the students.'

'They're jist beginners.'

'Not on your nelly! They're just useless. None of them can paint. It's sad but so true.'

'Too bad.'

'How would you like to model for me? Privately? Not a word to the others of course.'

Dolly looked around the room. The walls were covered with erotic paintings of beautiful girls. Girls like herself. She thought she saw her face on each voluptuous body.

'These,' he motioned, 'are pictures I've done in tribute to you. You, you see, are my ideal embodied in the most sensuous flesh. These pictures are how I imagine you. I've done it all from imagination. I've never come to your life classes: don't like the idea of sharing my vision with the duds. But I can see you — see you through your clothes.'

Dolly should have felt uncomfortable but didn't.   She felt flattered. She arched her back and pushed out her charming chest.   The Principal smiled, a smile of pure happiness.

'Would you do me the honour of modelling for me in my own home so I can make a proper job of painting you?'

'Sure,' said Dolly.   'Jist say the word.'

Lifting a rolled-gold pen the Principal wrote down his address on a piece of Ingres paper.   'Nine this evening?'

Dolly took the paper.   'Aye.   OK.'

Nine: Dolly Agonistes

Not in the clamour of the crowded street,
Not in the shouts and plaudits of the throng,
But in ourselves, are triumph and defeat.
Longfellow, 'The Poets'

Dolly was in for something of a shock that night at nine. She arrived punctually and found the Principal waiting for her with a glint in his eye.

'Drink dear?'

'Dinnae touch the stuff.'

'I've had a few, won't you join me?'

'Naw, 's no good for ma figure.'

The mention of 'figure' triggered him off.

'Renoir,' he began, 'used to.......'

'Eh? Rinwho?'

'Renoir, my dear, the French artist! Renoir used to say he painted with his penis rather than his brush. I am a follower of Renoir.'

At that he unzipped and presented her with his erect prick. She gasped. Not at the size of it (for virginal Dolly had no way of knowing the norm) but at the impudence of him.

'Pit that away,' she said reasonably enough.

'Come to me Dolly!'

'Nae bloody fear.'

The Principal walked awkwardly towards her, still gripping his weapon like a crusader ready to do battle. He got what was coming to him.

Dolly took aim and placed her sharply pointed patent-leather shoe underneath the Principal's offensive weapon and rammed her point home. The Principal shrieked. Dolly left with a flourish. Her days as a model were at an end. More than that she was profoundly, and traumatically, shocked.

Ten: The Education of Dolly

I would be married, but I'd have no wife,
I would be married to a single life.
    Richard Crashaw, 'On Marrriage'

Dolly was out of a job.   She wasn't too worried about that.   What really concerned her was her sudden antipathy to men.   She hated them all.   They only wanted one thing and that one thing she was unwilling to part with.   She would have to change her life again.

Dolly went to Mabel's flat and told her sad story.

'Aye, men are bastards Dolly.'

'Aye.'

'Lissen, it's aboot flamin time this wis a woman's world.'

'Aye.'

'Lissen, you and me should dae somethin about it, eh?'

Thus began the education of Dolly.   She resumed her job in the pub but her act was now cold and calculated.   Cool in execution and calculated to enmesh men.   She got them to do things for her, carry her bag, drive her here and there.   Always she denied them the thing they wanted.   And — they loved her all the more for being unattainable.

In the afternoons Dolly read.   She got a reader's ticket at a big reference library and consulted the bibliography of feminist literature. Within three weeks she had read every book on the subject.   She was an authority on female subjection was Dolly.

Eleven: To the Mainline Station

If ifs and ands were pots and pans
There'd be no work for the tinkers.
Thomas Love Peacock, 'Manley'

Dolly became an expert organiser. Rapidly she built up a devoted band of followers. Mabel was her righthand woman. The others were totally subservient to her.

Having commenced on her destiny she saw things through to a logical conclusion. Dolly would control the means of production. She formed a troupe of gogo dancers who could drive men mad. Once all men had been driven mad — Dolly reasoned — women would take over everything. And she meant everything.

It was a travelling troupe. They took their art to the people. They had their own private train, *The Cerebral Express,* and went from town to town with their outrageous art. Advance notices would go up, the word would spread, then *The Cerebral Express* would arrive. It was a silver train, womanned by forty beautiful girls. They would get off the train, and shake themselves about in time to preselected muzak. Men would stiffen, then wilt at the unattainability of it all. They became demoralised and dependent on Dolly. She was well on her way to becoming the most powerful woman in the country.

Twelve: The Great Divide

For men may come and men may go,
But I go on for ever.
Tennyson, 'The Brook'

It was a short road, really from home to the Capital. Dolly knew that when they arrived the revolution would be complete. Mankind would be enervated, reduced to a group of washouts. They could be easily manipulated. And, as *The Cerebral Express* moved through the country, so it took more broads on board. The Long Trip was a success. Dolly's Army was growing.

The day come when Dolly's party celebrated in the Capital. The revolution was, apparently, complete. Dolly announced as much to her followers.

174

Thirteen: Tomorrow And Tomorrow

For all sad words of tongue or pen,
The saddest are these: 'It might have been!'
John Greenleaf Whittier, 'Maud Muller'

That night Dolly embraced Mabel with all the love she was capable of. She, Dolly Silver, had brought men to her knees. As for the future — the sky was the limit.

'We've done no bad hen,' said Mabel that night.

'Aye.'

Uniform with this Volume
in
The Blew Blanket Library

Tall Tales From An Island
Peter Macnab
An intriguing medley of Tales from Mull — although they could
equally well have come from any one of the Hebrides or anywhere
in the Highlands.   Witches and Warlocks, lovers and liars, heroes
and headless horsemen all roar through these stories, which Peter
Macnab learned round the ceilidh-fires of his childhood.   He re-
tells them now in prose rich with the rythms of the Hebrides, and
shot through with strong love and deep compassion.

The Crofting Years
Francis Thompson
A deeply researched social history of crofting in the Highlands and
Islands.   In its short lifetime of one hundred years, the crofting
system of landholding has had profound effects upon Scotland and
the Scots.   Francis Thompson, a Gaelic scholar of high repute,
who lives in Stornoway, has written of crofting with intimate
knowledge.   His vivid descriptions of crofting life in the past and
now are essential for understanding modern Scotland.   This book
is no exercise in nostalgia for a dead past, but with restrained
passion and pity, Francis Thompson takes us into the homes and
the very minds of those who fought so desparately for security on
their land.   And he looks at, and fears for, the future.   This is no
dull book of history, but a chronicle, beautifully written, of a way of
life.